P9-AFW-491

Jelly

ALSO BY JACK ANSELL

His Brother, the Bear
The Shermans of Mannerville

Jelly

☼ ☼ ☼ ☼ ☼ ☼ ☼ ☼

A NOVEL BY

Jack Ansell

ARBOR HOUSE
NEW YORK

 Published in the United States by Arbor House Publishing Co., Inc., New York, and simultaneously in Canada by Nelson, Foster & Scott, Ltd.

FIRST EDITION

Library of Congress Catalog Card Number 75-167745
ISBN 0-87795-018-0

Manufactured in the United States of America

FOR ALL THOSE WHO BELIEVE,
AND THOSE WHO DON'T

Thou shalt love the Lord, thy God, with all thy heart, with all thy soul, and with all thy might. And these words, which I command thee this day, shall be upon thy heart. Thou shalt teach them diligently unto thy children, and shalt speak of them when thou sittest in thy house, when thou walkest by the way, when thou liest down, and when thou risest up. Thou shalt bind them for a sign upon thy hand, and they shall be for frontlets between thine eyes. Thou shalt write them upon the doorposts of thy house and upon thy gates: That ye may remember and do My commandments and be holy unto your God.

Thou shalt love . . .

Jelly

Part One

☼ ☼ ☼ ☼ ☼ ☼ ☼ ☼

CHAPTER ONE

It was during an evening service for Yom Kippur, the Day of Atonement, in the crowded sanctuary of Temple B'nai Israel on St. Charles Street in New Orleans, that Jacob ("Jack") Weiss, thirty-six, B'nai Israel's rabbi for just under three years, made his decision. It happened so quickly, so simply, so solemnly and irrevocably, that for some minutes he didn't realize how tumultuously the weight of months, perhaps years, had been lifted from his shoulders; his chest. It happened during a responsive reading.

"O Thou, Who hearest prayer, unto Thee shall all flesh come," he had just intoned in his rich, vibrant voice, and the congregation was responding with "All flesh shall come to worship before Thee, O Lord, and to do honor to Thy name," when the voice that spoke next, while still unmistakably his own—"With Thee is the fountain of life; in Thy light do we see light"—was not the voice that he heard. The voice that he heard—even as the congregation in its prescribed tradition came in heartily on cue: "Thy righteousness is an everlasting righteousness, and Thy law is truth"—was the voice he had suppressed for time out of mind:

Just a few more hours. A few more hours and I'll no longer be a rabbi.

"Listen to the voice of my supplication, my King and my God, for to Thee do I pray."

No longer a rabbi. No longer having to say what I no longer believe. No longer having to do . . .

"Give ear to my words, O Lord, have regard to my prayer," said the congregation.

"Lead me, O Lord, in Thy righteousness, make Thy path straight before me," he said.

Path straight to you, Jelly, path straight to you.

"Lead me, O Lord, in Thy righteousness, make Thy path straight before me," said the congregation.

"Order my steps by Thy word; let not iniquity have dominion over me," he replied.

I am leaving you, too, Miriam.

"Turn away mine eyes from beholding vanity, and quicken me in Thy ways," said the congregation.

"Deliver me in Thy righteousness and rescue me; incline Thine ear unto me and save me," he said.

Save me? Save me from what? From Jelly? From Jelly's arms, Jelly's . . .?

"In Thee did our fathers trust," insisted the congregation; "in Thee did they trust and were not ashamed."

Nor am I! Nor am I ashamed!

The choir sang now: "Prepare to meet Thy God, O Israel! Seek ye the Lord and ye shall live. Let justice flow forth as water, and righteousness as a mighty stream."

Jacob listened; heard. But mainly he saw. The summer-worn faces of the congregation. *His* congregation. The Mark Weinsteins. The Lou Broders. The Saul Rosenbergs. The Clifford Blooms. Miss Mattie Bernstein. Miss Sadie Meyer. Joe Mintz. Miriam.

The Barrons, the Lilienthals, the Lowensteins, the Kaplans. Miriam. . . .

"Be gracious unto me, O God, according to Thy loving-kindness," he said; half-sang.

"In Thine endless mercy, blot out my transgressions," the congregation sang back.

"Cleanse me, O Lord, and I shall be clean; purify me and I shall be whiter than snow."

"Behold Thou desirest truth in our innermost heart; so teach me wisdom and right understanding."

Truth in our innermost heart. Yes. Your truth, Jelly. Your truth. Your . . .

"I acknowledge my transgressions and my sin is ever before me."

"Create in me a clean heart, O God, renew a steadfast spirit within me," said the congregation.

"Cast me not away from Thy presence and take not Thy holy spirit from me," said he in turn.

And they: "The soul is Thine and the body is Thine; O have compassion in Thy handiwork."

And he: "For Thee, O Lord, do we wait; in Thee, O Lord, do we hope, for with the Lord there is mercy and with Him is plenteous redemption."

Redemption. I know I should ask this of you, Miriam. I know I should, but . . .

The choir sang again. The service dragged on. It was during the last response before the sermon—

"Our Father, our King, we have sinned before Thee."

"Our Father, our King, inscribe us for blessing in the book of life."

—that he knew with any real degree of certainty how certain he was.

Your book of life, Jelly. Your big, beautiful, endless book of life!

The choir sang (interminably), "Amen." He began his sermon: "On this holiest of days, as there is a rebellious world to remind us, we must go back to the beginning, back to why we are here in such numbers today, why this day of all days, this night of all nights . . ."

He took for his text Chapter 16 of Leviticus, which begins, "And the Lord spoke unto Moses after the death of the two sons of Aaron, when they offered before the Lord, and died; and the Lord said unto Moses, Speak unto Aaron thy brother, that he come not at all times into the holy place within the vail before the mercy seat, which is upon the ark, that he die not . . . ," and ends, "And this shall be an everlasting statute unto you, to make an atonement for the children of Israel, for all their sins, once a year. And he did as the Lord commanded Moses." And Jacob could tell by the great collective sigh that it was the most affecting sermon he had ever delivered.

They walked home, as the Day of Atonement commands. It was milky hot, mosquito hot, as New Orleans in September commands. St. Charles Street was lazy with the sweet, sickly thickness of it, impregnated here and there by river smells and the fragrances of hyacinth and phlox. The avenue itself, even at night and darker than usual, looked white-hot, its faded old houses with their French iron-lace balconies and Victorian gables and Georgian façades and colonial columns (still incongrously charming) a blinding oneness as far as the eye could see. The small lawns, though starting to turn their reluctant October brown, looked white as well, and luminous; as though the stars, in celebration of a whim, were sprinkling them all with sequins. Jacob found it difficult to breathe.

"You were very distinguished tonight," said the woman at his side, a little robin of a woman, frail and pink, with very thin legs and a sharp beak of a nose. When she smiled, though rarely, it too turned pink, if a darker, more somber tone.

Jacob nodded in the night, not knowing if she saw him, saying nothing.

"Very," she said, not so much to him or to herself as to the night.

It was a long walk. The stately old avenue was virtually void of pedestrians, although traffic was unusually heavy. Occasionally someone would pass them, breathing heavily the gumbo air, silently cursing the errand that had brought him out on such a humid evening. Once, one of the congregants and his family, Sidney Feldstein, passed them in their new Buick on their way up St. Charles, waving and shouting, "You were right on the button tonight, Rabbi," while a smaller voice from the rear called out, "Groovy, Rabbi, groovy." The congregants, being Reform Jews, always rode on the Sabbath. He and Miriam, though long part of, and advocates of, Reform ways, still walked, carried no money on them, and fasted on Yom Kippur.

It took them almost forty minutes to reach Poydras Street, where they turned left toward the imposing dwelling that another of his congregants, Mark Weill, had turned from his family's turn-of-the-century mansion into a six-family apartment house. The rabbi's high-ceiling four-room apartment with its dullish white walls still contained several of the original antiques, most of which had since been sold at auction. Two overstuffed armchairs laden with antimacassars in the living room, an old English highboy in the dining room, an elaborate trunk-cedar chest in the master bedroom, a hand-carved Oriental caramandel in the den-study: they were graphically at odds with the plain Colonial furniture that Miriam had inherited from her mother.

The kitchen, on the other hand, was very contemporary and very functional. And very bright. Jacob made straight for it. And if there was even a second's hesitation when he opened the door to the refrigerator it wasn't discernible. He broke off the leg and thigh of a chicken Miriam had boiled earlier in the day to break their fast at sundown tomorrow, and gazing thoughtfully across the room where she stood in the doorway, began delicately but decisively to eat it. Her own face, while outwardly expressionless, could hardly conceal the icy one behind it.

"Yes," he said, "On Yom Kippur."

Her thin lips scarcely moved. "It's come to this?" slipped sibilantly between them.

Slowly, he answered her: "I'm afraid it has, Miriam. I'm afraid it has come to this."

CHAPTER TWO

Shema Yisroel Adonoi Elohenu
Adonoi Echod. Boruch Shem
Khevod Melechuso L'Eolom Voed . . .

Small child, large voice, larger than any of them, rising to the beams of the *shul* ceiling in the sweet round tones of love. First love.

"He has such fineness of heart, my Jacob."

"Yahweh looks benevolently upon him."

Always, since the hour of time, it had been that way.

"I love God, Mama. God's big. God's bigger than Howie Epstein's dog. Howie Epstein's dog is cute but he don't talk. God talks."

"I talked to God again last night, Papa. He told me Howie Epstein's a schmuck."

Spanked, hide tanned (in Dallas even the Orthodox were assimilated; within bounds)—God was right. Howie Epstein *was* a schmuck.

You would have to have known Howie Epstein. Fat, balding (even at twelve years old), he had an imperious manner that seems to be the special province of rich, ugly children. "You really believe all this hocus pocus, don't you, Jake? *Shul* and *Shanos* and *Sefira* and *Sukos* and *Simkhas Torah*? Well, I put 'em all together under one big S. Shit. That's all they are. And I can't wait for the day I take this stupid-looking skullcap off my head forever and tell my sweet gentle papa to stick it up his Talmud-loving ass!" Jacob hated Howie Epstein.

And loved, *loved,* God.

It was not easy to explain and he never tried to. How explain to anyone, much less Howie Epstein, the very personal presence that was always with him, that spoke with him not just in dreams but awake, wide awake, at morning and at night and in all the private times between? How speak aloud of the secret things—the unquestionable knowing that Sin and Salvation were the least of it; that Scholarship was the way to His grace?

His glory.

Jacob couldn't recall a day when he hadn't studied; read; pored over Torah passages until his eyes bled; even explored, albeit unsurely, both the Mishna and Gemara of the Talmud. His Hebrew schooling, while in Dallas leaving much to be desired, had been arduous at least—on his part anyway. His prayers were fluent, an infinite storehouse, and if his Aramaic was sketchy he fairly excelled with the Hebrew Bible. He was also exceptionally good in English at Sam Houston High School. His father, who ran a prosperous chain of delicatessens in the greater metropolitan area but had once dreamed of becoming a cantor, looked upon him with near-embarrassing pride. His brother, Samuel, who was several years older and already working part-time in one of the delicatessens, held him in equal awe.

"Papa . . . Mama . . . they love both of us, Jacob. But they'll never be as proud of me as they are of you. I'll be a good businessman, I know. Papa knows it, too. But his eyes won't ever light up over the neat books I keep, not like they light up when you read from the Torah . . . the Talmud. You're very special, Jacob. I'm real proud you're my brother. Real proud, Jacob."

His friends, too—Howie Epstein notwithstanding—made of him something special, too.

"Old Jack's a regular guy"—from Dick Friedman, who was something of a twelve-year-old wit—"but if he's got one foot in Dallas, the other's sure as shootin up 'air playin footsie with The Man. Whooee!"

It was just before his bar mitzvah, when both accomplishment and anticipation shone as jewels from his eyes, that he began to keep a journal, which he titled *Notes To and Upon My Creator.* During the next few years he would become more and more amused by its outright presumptuousness (what rational boy, after all, keeps a running dialogue with God?), but it was to remain with him, at his fingertips, volumes in fact, until that bitter day in the St. Peter Street apartment in New Orleans.

February 16. Soon I shall be a man, they say. Approaching manhood in the sight of my elders is a momentous thing. But not to compare with what it might be in Your sight. I just made that up.

February 17. Papa has brought me home a new book called Man and God. *There is much in it I admire. On page 57 there is a quotation from Rabbi Elineleph of Lizheusk that I want to remember: It is good if man can bring about that God sings within him.*

March 11. Through Rabbi Simonson I have discovered Martin Buber. There is one passage—"God is divided into two, through the created world and its actions. He is divided into the ultimate being of God, Elohut, which is remote and apart from the creatures, and the Presence of God, his Glory, the Shekhina, which dwells in the world, wandering astray and scattered." I am not sure I understand this. I guess I'm hard shelled. The Lord our God, the Lord is One.

April 20. As You know, I hit Howie Epstein's fat face for You today. I hope You weren't intimidated.

May 4. It was more than my bar mitzvah. It was the supreme day of my life. Thank You.

It was at about this time that he began toying with the idea of becoming a rabbi. His father's encouragement, of course, was paramount in these early ruminations, unusual in that Solomon Weiss had five delicatessens but only two sons.

"For Sammy it's the business, Jacob; he's got the head for figures. For Sammy it's the ledger books. But for you, my Jacob, for you . . . Ah, the books of another kind. For you, my Jacob, the books of life, the books of God. . . ."

But if his father influenced him greatly in his ultimate decision, no less a mentor of his soul (rather ethereally, he liked to think of it as that) was Rabbi Chaim Rostok, a tall, muscular, altogether powerful old man with a great head of stone-gray hair and a formidable gray beard, who surely of all men must have been created in His image. Through all of Jacob's years of study Reb Rostok counseled him with a kind of arch devotion, a stern seriousness sweetened by kind humor.

"A rabbi, a teacher of men, this you shall be, Yakov (*Yakov, always Yakov*). I know it, I feel it. In my heart, this poor old heart, I feel it. You have a good speaking voice, Yakov, and a fine singing voice, and a mind rich with good thoughts and dedication. Besides, you have a streak of the rebel in you too. A rabbi is by nature a traditionalist but in an age of spiritual vapidness his love of God also makes him something of a rebel. And besides, besides. What is selling kosher chickens compared with *pronouncing* them kosher?"

Rabbi Chaim Rostok's death in Jacob's sixteenth year marked his first great loss, his first real sense of loss.

It was during his senior year at Sam Houston, when he had become friendly—through the school's baseball team—with several boys from a Reform congregation (which his father still thought of as goyim) that Jacob settled upon the Reform rabbinate, rather than the Orthodox or even Conservative, for a career. It was not an easy decision. But despite a preoccupation with prayer and study, the occasional delights of a Texas boyhood were not entirely lost on him. The world in fact was very much with him. He excelled in sports, particularly baseball; he became an Eagle Scout; he was more than a little aware of, and attracted to, girls (those he went out with, of course, were necessarily Jewish, and as everyone knew—or at least everyone *said*—nice Jewish girls *never*—and through the perseverence of prayer and a heavy schedule of cold showers, neither did he); and he spent hours, secretly, reading popular novels, and on the piano playing popular songs.

(On the piano playing popular songs. In his senior year at Sam Houston the rebel in him surfacing and through a challenge, a dare, from a peripheral friend known as Attaboy Bates—shortstop on the baseball team, and, in Solomon Weiss's world, very much the uncircumcized heathen—whose cousin played a piano and sang at a North Side club called the Lazy Longhorn, catering mainly to teenagers—through a challenge, a dare, to sit in for a week for the cousin, who had acute laryngitis, making his first professional (pagan) appearance. Playing and singing—all the popular songs of the day: "Tennessee Waltz" and "From Rags to Riches" and "Wheel of Fortune" and "Secret Love" and an occasional standard—"Deep Purple," "Stardust"—relishing every minute of it, oddly buoyed by applause and his own virtuosity, even if guilt-ridden at having to lie to his father about the long, late nights at the school and *shul* libraries. In some way drawn, as no religious scholar should be, to the lilt and the lift and the laughter. Then, on the third night, in the middle of "Deep in the Heart of Texas," his father and brother Sam standing in the small entranceway, less anger than disappointment on their good, sad faces. Accompanying them home, shamed tail between his legs, no word uttered, no look exchanged. Yet in the early morning hours, in a troubled half-sleep, a half-singing bird—his father, a very frail man, was not so far from that—"You got responsibilities, Jacob. Responsibilities to your people. Responsibilities these yokels around here don't know from a *knish.* Responsibilities that go back for thousands of years, responsibilities that don't allow no compromise, Jacob . . .")

Still, compromise, in a way, was the way he knew he had to go. As he rationalized it in his journal, *I am of two worlds, but I believe, I truly believe, that I can serve best in a contemporary one. I know in my heart this will not offend God. Of course it's going to send Papa to bed.*

"Better you should tell me you was going to be a Russian spy than a goy preacher."

"Papa, this is America in the twentieth century. The old ways have to blend with the new. And it's not as if I myself won't continue to observe the Laws. It's just a question of communication, Papa. That's all. Communication. Besides, I think it's what God wants me to do."

"So! You're still in direct personal communication with God, hah? Putting words in God's mouth, that's what you're doing!"

"Someday you'll understand, Papa."

"Someday I'll drop dead."

"Marry a girl keeps a kosher home," said his mother, patting his head.

He met her at a Purim festival in Cincinnati during his last year at Hebrew Union College. She was there with her father, the retiring rabbi of Temple Beth Elohem in Springfield, Georgia, who had been dispatched by his congregation to survey the year's bright new crop for a likely successor. And it was he, Jacob, with his Texas background, who appeared (at least in preliminary inquiry) to have been tapped.

She was a quiet girl, Miriam Zimmerman, and plain by any of the several sexual standards, but relentlessly alert and pridefully kosher. Even in the southern environs in which her father had served for some forty years, she had kept a faultlessly pure house and preserved as many of the old ways as was practical. (She had been a late child and her mother had died when she was ten.)

She was a studious girl. Study and faith were physically embedded in the contour of her long, rather bony face. Even in that brief weekend they spoke together of the Koran as well as the Talmud (from which she could quote whole passages), not to mention Kierkegaard and Freud and Marx, and before she departed Cincinnati, she kissed him and let him touch one of her small, hereto untouched breasts. Over the next few months, while settling into his Springfield, Georgia, pulpit—no simple task, it being not only his first (aside from practice services on the High Holidays in small towns without rabbis, which Hebrew Union College arranged) but one dominated so long by one man, one voice—over the next few months he saw a great deal of her.

They went to movies together, and concerts at Town Hall, and dinner at one of the three or four acceptable restaurants in Springfield, and he was invariably her escort for dinner at congregants' homes. They were at ease with each other, and kind.

And safe.

"I'm glad neither of us has ever . . . well, you know, Jacob . . . *had* relations of that . . . *that* sort. It makes our own relationship more . . . more special. You feel that way too, don't you Jacob?"

Did he? He didn't dare ask himself. Already a vague sense of disappointment, of disillusionment, with the rabbinate itself had begun to gnaw at him; sex, fulfillment from sex, were the last things he needed to think about. Besides: kissing her goodnight, pressing against her, exploring even decorously the alien parts of her, he did feel a stirring of sorts in his groin, a pinch in his chest, that surely were just this side of desire.

He debated at length with himself over what he felt, didn't feel. There was, after all, a somewhat limited history for comparison. Then one night, after a rather intense discussion of the myriad Hebraic interpretations of God, both ancient and modern (and not unlike similar discussions with his classmates at HUC, those long nights when intellect confronted emotion, and doubt itself came perilously close to torture, only to be sublimated by thoughts of his father and Reb Rostok and deep, redemptive study), and several glasses of wine at The Embers, Springfield's most elegant restaurant; a night, too, when her father was at an annual Kiwanis barbecue; the rebel in him surfaced as never before and he touched her fully in the most sacred Jewish-girl place of all.

"Jacob," she sighed, frightened but at the same time certain it would go no further. "Ah, Jacob, Jacob. Dear, dear Jacob."

Safe.

In less than a year he asked her to marry him. He hadn't so much fallen in love with her as he'd fallen in thought with her, and in the word "helpmeet" he found both a spiritual and intellectual satisfaction.

They were married not in Springfield but in Dallas, in a traditional Orthodox ceremony, and with both her father and Rabbi Simonson officiating. His own father, long resigned simply to muttering "*Oy is ehi uh yuld.* A donkey, my sow. A sweet donkey but still a donkey" was hard put to conceal an open smile, and his mother literally wept for joy.

It was a union blessed. Both were very serious, and

very dedicated, and very virginal, and they each had nervous stomachs, which were also blessed, and while he in some strange restiveness tended to be somewhat orbital —never quite satisfied with where he was or what he was doing—and she somewhat grounded, they were unquestionably the Rabbi and his Wife.

More, they were friends.

And there was God. Whoever, Whatever, Yahweh, Yisroel, He was with them, beside them, between them.

Very much between them. Nights and early mornings, particularly, were witness to not the most artful of conjugal delights.

Still, Jacob found pleasure in her; or thought he did.

They remained with Congregation Beth Elohem in Springfield for five years (her father and his mother passing on in the fourth of them), then moved on (restively, on his part) to Congregation B'nai Jeremiah and Congregation Massas Benjamin in small Texas towns, and Congregation Rodeph Sholom in a suburb of Chicago, and Congregation Isaiah in Mannerville, Louisiana. It was there that he met Jo Ellen Johnson—Jelly; and began his undreamed-of infraction, his helpless deflection from the ways of his father.

CHAPTER THREE

"It's a very dramatic gesture," she said. "The thigh of a chicken negates a lifetime."

"Yes," he said.

It was very warm in the small kitchen, warmer even than the New Orleans night beyond it, but on the Sabbath Miriam frowned upon air conditioning. A light layer of perspiration ringed her mouth like dew upon mountain rock.

"I'm not sure you disappoint me even," she said. "It's too like what a rebellious child might do. You simply tire me, Jacob." She had never addressed him other, even though he had been called "Jack" throughout his years at the University of Cincinnati and Hebrew Union College and by most personal congregants since. Except by her father and Aunt Corinne, and of course his own father and brother Sam.

"I suppose an end to something always has the trace

of a child's rebellion," he said. There was something of a child's sadness, as well, in his full man's voice.

She tried to smile, but it was painfully dour. "Can the rebellious child spell out exactly what he's trying to tell me?"

The piece of chicken, suspended in mid-air between them, looked less a symbol of rebellion then Jeremiah's prophet's staff. "I won't have you indulging me, Miriam. That I will not have. There is nothing and no one here to indulge. It's as simple as G-O-D. I'm leaving the rabbinate."

"For what? To do what?"

"To breathe," he said. "We sigh a lot, Miriam. We rarely breathe."

"You never loved me, did you, Jacob?" she said; asked, without expression or apparent emotion.

He looked away, not so much evading her eyes as denying their existence. "We're speaking of the rabbinate, Miriam."

"And God," she said.

"Yes. And God."

"*A man of God!*" Her voice now was at its highest pitch, and unrestrained, as if yanked from her mouth like an aching tooth.

Thoughtfully, he pulled back a chair from the vinyl-top kitchen table and sank with a kind of deliberate slowness into it. "A man, Miriam. Simply a man," he said.

"And God is dead"—an edginess now, just short of a sneer—"the cliché of an age. It's not worthy of you, Jacob."

"Your words, not mine," he said, not looking up. "That's hardly what's at issue."

"Oh? And what is at issue, Jacob?" Still standing, but more visibly controlled.

He did look up now, gently meeting her eyes. "Man himself," he said softly. "You know that. How many times must we go through this? I just can't go on intellectualizing and rationalizing and making brilliantly complex what's so agonizingly simple. Either you believe or you don't believe. And all the King's men are just hypocritical ornaments if the King himself isn't there. Not all the theology in the world can supplant truth. Or what one single man, microcosm that he is, divines as truth."

"Glib, Jacob," she said, "very glib. The single most imaginative, provocative, disturbing confrontation of mankind and you dismiss it in fifteen seconds. You who have spent a lifetime in study and sanctification—yes, *sanctification*—talking like a pseudo-intellectual sophomore. God isn't a teddy bear, Jacob. You don't discard Him simply because one day you discover you're a big boy."

"Miriam! Please! You know what I've gone through to reach this moment, now . . ."

She turned away. "We shouldn't have moved around so much. We didn't always need more money, more benefits, not that much."

"It wasn't just better contracts. I was restless. You know that. It was happening even then."

"It happened in Mannerville."

He stiffened. "A thing like this doesn't happen in a *place*, Miriam," he said; avoiding still her eyes. "The place is the mind, the heart, the human spirit . . . whatever you choose to call it. A physical place, an environment, is merely . . ."

"It happened in Mannerville."

He stood; wearily. "What's the use? I'm very tired."

"In Mannerville. Her."

If his voice was somewhat sharp, he had little control over it. "Miriam, that's absurd and you know it. That was something that . . ."

"She's here, isn't she? The *shikse* tramp. She's in New Orleans. I know it. I know she's here . . ." While not exactly hysterical she was tense to the point of tears. "I feel it, I sense it . . ."

Taking another bite of the chicken—not defiantly so much as guiltily—he said, "It's a long day tomorrow, Miriam. A very long day. I'm very tired."

She sank, simply sank. "Maybe if we'd had children . . ."

"That's irrelevant, too," he said.

Drearily, by rote, she cleared the small sin from the table, muttering, almost to herself, "*Gam zu l'tovah*"—

May all this be to the good.

Somewhere in the night her hand covered his and she said, "What will you do, Jacob?"

"Write, for one thing," he said; thought he said. "About this. Yes, this, I think."

Barely breath. "How will we live?"

His hand didn't move. "I want you to go to your Aunt Corinne's in Louisville," he said. "For a while. Perhaps a long while. I'm going to stay in New Orleans, Miriam. For a while."

Her hand left.

Her voice was faint in the darkness. "There's something my father used to say. When a man turns his back on something good, it's his front that's shamed."

But he didn't say anything and somehow the night passed, they slept.

CHAPTER FOUR

The Day of Atonement passed somehow, too. The morning service went smoothly, the choir was in splendid voice, his own voice was even and controlled. In the early morning he had decided not to deliver his announced sermon, "The Unvanishing Jew" (taken from Isaiah: *In those days ten men from the nations of every tongue shall take hold of the robe of a Jew, saying, "Let us go with you, for we have heard that God's with you"*) and switched instead to one he had given in Chicago, based on Maurice Eisendrath's contention that the American synagogue has become increasingly a blend of Jewish country club and Protestant church. With even this, inwardly, he was very uncomfortable, but his delivery, he knew, was faultless.

Both the afternoon and memorial services, as well as the concluding one, were all equally smooth, and in the late afternoon, after sounding the shofar, he announced to the few congregants remaining that he would be leaving not only Temple B'nai Israel but the rabbinate as well. Then, in the gasping silence and far above Miriam's eyes, he began the final prayers—

"Va-anachnu koreem umishtachaveem umodeem, lifnay melech malchay hamlocheem, hakodosh boruch hu."

(We bow the head in reverence, and worship the King of Kings, the Holy One, praised be He.)

"Shema Yisroel Adonoi Elohenu . . ."

Afterward—to avoid the personal greetings, and today, the questions (he hadn't informed either the Board or the president of the congregation of what he had just announced)—he remained for some time in his study just off the rostrum, having asked Miriam to say he was seeing no one. When finally Miriam joined him, after the last of the congregants had departed, she simply stood in front of one of the floor-to-ceiling bookcases where scores of old titles in chipped fading gold stood their ground among the new ones on blatant bright dust jackets and said, "Don't come home with me, Jacob. I want to break fast alone. Today at least. Please." He nodded, and tried hard to smile his understanding, but she was gone so quickly that he doubted she saw it.

Bourbon Street in the French Quarter is at dusk a special kind of purgatory, particularly on a humid day. The circus lights and sounds are still an hour or so away, and while the fabled architecture is still proudly on view, it is a melancholy view. The delicate wrought-iron lace of the fine old balconies looks almost as weary from the hot day as the day's tourists. The restless natives in any number aren't yet aroused. Those who are, are mostly young and in clusters, for whatever the time of day, for them the street is the big party of home.

Driving the length of it (if one can be said to drive on Bourbon; "walking your tires" is more appropriate in this narrow lane), Jacob was only dimly aware of the almost innocent flirtation with sin that batted its eyes at him from either side: Galatea, the Statue That Comes to Life; Sheila, Miss Boobs; Sandra Sexton; Kitten's Den; the Red Garter; Hoitsy Toitsy; Renée Latouse, the Langorous Lioness; Papa Pete's Playthings; Gays and Dolls—all unabashedly at home and at peace with the New Orleans Po-Bay stands and the Oyster bars and the hamburger joints and Orange Julius; and the Old Absinthe House and the Original Absinthe House and Galatoire's and the Vieux Carré Restaurant and the L'Esplanade Café and Café Creole; and the 809 Club and Al Hirt's 500 Club and Dixieland Hall; and the antique shops and candy stores and art galleries and hotels. Jacob saw, and was excited by, none of them today. It seemed hours before he reached the corner of St. Peter and, turning right, off Bourbon at last, maneuvered the embarrassingly long Oldsmobile (gift of Congregation B'nai Israel) into an impossible parking space.

The house was French Colonial, at least a century old, not unlike the others on St. Peter (or St. Ann or Bienville or St. Louis or Toulouse), its handmade iron lace gracing three narrow balconies. Her apartment was on the third, the top, floor.

She stood in the doorway, the room behind her its usual shambles. She was a tall girl, large, ridiculously healthy, shamefully tanned; twenty-three at the most. Her straight blonde hair reached defiantly to her waist, her eyes were a light sea-green, and she wore nothing but a man's tank shirt sizes too large for her. And before Jacob could say anything, or think to say anything, she was upon him like a playful dolphin, and he found his way to her like a fish to water, and her mouth on his ear was a shell song.

"Oh you marvelous man, you simply marvelous man! Oh you lovely super groovy *darlin* rabbi!"

Part Two

☼ ☼ ☼ ☼ ☼ ☼ ☼ ☼

CHAPTER FIVE

THE CRESCENT CAROUSEL
APPEARING NIGHTLY
JACK WHITE
King of the Keyboard,
Sorceror of Song

Jacob paused, smiled, half-smiled, as he did every time he passed the billboard with its glossy photograph of him in a blue tuxedo, nested in a silver frame at the Royal Street club's entrance. Then, widening the smile—still somewhat timidly—he made his entrance.

It was a small room—"the most intimate in the Quarter," its owner, Joe Capella, called it in his newspaper ads. At least three-quarters of it was taken up by a revolving piano bar, which in truth was its chief attraction. Only seven booths, seductively darkened, occupied the rest. They, along with the bar stools, were already half filled.

"You're late again, Reb," Capella (a short, fat, aging

Italian who looked peculiarly like Peter Lorre) growled under his breath, intercepting him in the tiny foyer. Jacob winced, if inwardly. *Reb.* Three months and he was still uptight about it. But then coming to see the ex-rabbi who played piano and sang sentimental songs was "the thing to do" in New Orleans these days, particularly for the square set. He countered under his own breath, "Count your blessings, friend," and made his way, amid sporadic applause, to the piano.

Where he began, with a modesty now becoming a trademark along the immodest Quarter streets, to tune up.

"If Ever I Would Leave You," said a forty-odd woman with brown hair and browner eyes, sitting alone with a Sazerac, the two stools on either side of her conspicuously unoccupied. Jacob knew her, if not her name. She came in often. The Crescent Carousel, however sedate and discreet, was a great place for aging singles to meet. He smiled but continued toying with the keys.

"Autumn Leaves," said another woman, younger, blonder, obviously more secure with a well-dressed graying escort beside her.

"Impossible Dream," belched the man on her other side; large, slightly limp-wristed, dreamily drunk.

Jacob acknowledged them all with an appreciative nod, pulling himself closer to the white baby grand for his first set. Then starting softly to play, sing—

Raindrops keep falling on my head

—while the bar made its slow, seductively programmed revolutions.

At the end of the number there was the usual scattered, subdued applause, and he followed it with "Dream a Little

Dream of Me" and "Love Is a Many Splendored Thing" and "The Glory of Love" and "If We Only Have Love," finally tackling at least two of the requests—"Moon River" and "Autumn Leaves"—trying to tell the chagrined fag, with a promising shake of his head, that "Impossible Dream," like "Sunrise, Sunset," came at the end of a set, not the middle. A professional, after all, was a professional.

What kind of fool am I . . .

"Swingin. Real swingin."

Jacob smiled to himself. She often wandered in near the end of the first set, to have a drink with him during the brief intermission. Tonight she was particularly casual, in very old, very worn sailor slacks. He finished the set with a very dramatic "Impossible Dream."

"I'd love to bite your ass right now," she said, fingering a bourbon and water in one of the darkened booths. "Just bite bite bite bite bite."

"Jelly, you'll destroy me yet," he said, laughing in spite of himself. "You'll really destroy me yet." Looking for a moment at her, then beyond her, beyond the booth, the club; beyond years.

Beyond years.

"These are the rewarding years, Jacob," Miriam had said, on their very first day in Mannerville. "I hope we don't fragment them again, I hope we're not rash again, moving just for the sake of moving again. I don't even know this town but I hope it's home."

He had smiled, vaguely, and said, "I hope so, Miriam. I devoutly hope so." Not daring to express to her the uncomfortable truth, that Mannerville was simply another stop on a long trip to nowhere, that he was not at all comfortable in his role as rabbi. Confiding instead to his journal, *How does it happen, where does it begin? All your life you're prepared, prepped, for everything you are, everything you have, and then being it, having it, you discover for no reason on earth that you're rejecting it, resenting it, Papa and Reb Rostok notwithstanding, and you can't say why, can't know why. Except that Sisterhood luncheons and Men's Club suppers and Youth Group outings and . . . festivals, marriages, births, deaths . . . and . . . Dare I think it, much less write it? That, like a silly sophomore, I'm having doubts about the whole fabric of organized religion, of religious life, of . . . ,* not able to finish what he knew would be even more sophomoric, a confused, tumescent prose.

"I do so hope Mannerville is home," she said again.

And perhaps it would have been had not the girl (*girl!*) come to his office at Temple Isaiah that day, that late, lackluster November day; and smiled impishly or impudently; both. It had lasted no more than four minutes, five; a put-on so incredibly transparent that even the most unsophisticated, most naïve . . .

He hadn't forgotten a word of it.

"Hi."

"Hello."

"You're supposed to say 'Can I help you?' or 'Were you wantin somethin? or some such crap as that. Ain't you? —I'm sorry—*aren't* you?"

"Well. I suppose you're right. In my own phraseology of course. How about . . . May I be of service, young lady?"

"Lord. Studs say that."

"I . . . I . . . well. Well then, perhaps . . ."

"It's okay, Rabbi. Don't let me bug you. I'll make it snap crackle and pop. My name's Jo Ellen Johnson. Unless you don't go for that 'What's in a name' jazz? Anyway, everybody calls me Jelly. You'd know why if you didn't have to wear such stuffy suits. Anyway, I happened to be at your thing, service I mean, last Friday night. You know? With my friend Shirley Goldstein. I'd never been in a Jew church before and I was curious. I'm always curious about religious mess. I guess you can afford to be when you're just amused and not moved by any of it. My daddy's a Baptist preacher, you know. Reverend Josephus Johnson, over in South Mannerville? Anyway, I told him one night last week how sick it all was, religion I mean, and so naturally he had himself a divine inspiration and beat the shit out of me. Want to see the bruises?"

"I . . . well . . . no."

"Do I shock you?"

"I . . . no."

"Hey, you're cooler than I thought."

"Oh? And what was I . . . what was I supposed to be?"

"I don't know. Self-righteous and indignant maybe. Or real sweet and fatherly and full of piss and understanding. I'm crazy about four-letter words, you know."

"I know."

"Crazy *period,* I'll bet you're thinkin."

"You haven't the remotest idea what I'm thinking. Why . . . why are you here, Miss Johnson?"

"Maybe I dig Jew services. Maybe I think they're groovy."

"I doubt it."

"Maybe I'm just a smartass. Rebellin against the Establishment and all that pisseroo. Not many of *them* in Mannerville, you know."

"Perhaps."

"Boy! You really *are* playin it cool, ain't you? *Aren't* you?"

"Why did you come here, Miss Johnson?"

"Oh . . . maybe it's because you got a nice voice. 'May the Lord bless your comin out and your goin in' . . . or maybe it's because you're nice lookin. In that silly old mature kind of way of course."

"Thank you. I'm . . . flattered."

"Cool, real cool. We'll see each other again, you know. Maybe we'll even talk about . . . God. Big *G*, little *g*. Groovy, hunh, Rabbi?"

He had laughed; he couldn't help it. Her breezy femme fatale—one second, Lolita; the next, Mae West—had been beguiling, and even in the moment's bewilderment he was somehow touched.

In the weeks that followed the little charade there had been a pinprick here and there; the way she'd stood, cocked her head, challenged him with her eyes. But they were busy weeks for a rabbi in a new community, particularly one where the synagogue *(temple;* Rabbi, *please!)* —as Rabbi Eisendrath had put it—was half country club and half Methodist church. Besides his sermons and speaking engagements throughout Shamatau Parish, there was Hanukkah and a Youth Group outing and a dreary, unwelcome visit from Miriam's Aunt Corinne in Louisville. Then, during Christmas week, he had had to fly to Dallas, where his father was undergoing major stomach surgery. So, while the strange girl was not forgotten, she did recede, and it wasn't until the middle of January that she invaded his full consciousness again. That is, invaded his office again; as boldly and blithely as before.

"Surprised, Rabbi?"

"Not really."

"Pleased?"

"I hope we're not going through this again, Miss . . . ?"

"Jelly. Just Jelly."

"Jelly."

"Lord. You *are* good lookin. Not that I'd forgotten, but, well, I *have* been busy."

"I see. Now, what was it you . . . ?"

"I'm really out of sight, right?"

"Hardly. I can't imagine you ever being *out* of sight at anytime, Miss . . ."

"Jelly."

"Yes. Jelly."

"I'm makin you uncomfortable, right? You're squirmy, uptight. Right?"

"Look, Miss . . . Jelly. Look. I don't know what it is you . . ."

"Help, Rabbi. That's all. Just a little old simple cotton pickin help."

"Well, of course, if that's . . . How can I be of help . . . Jelly?"

"I can't talk about it here."

"Of course you can. There's nobody . . ."

"I said I can't talk about it here."

"I see."

"No, you don't. You don't see at all. You don't see anything. None of you do. Ever. None of you pissy preachers with your goddern pious . . ."

"What is it, Jelly? What is it you want?"

"Well, you *could* . . ."

"Yes, Jelly?"

"My folks ain't—*aren't*—goin to be home next Wednesday night. Daddy's doin a silly revival thing over in Rayville. I could talk freer there. I mean, I wouldn't feel so gauche there. At the house I mean. Three eleven Wood Street in South Mannerville, two blocks east of the O.K. Allen Bridge. I feel I'd at least have a little territorial *imperative* there. That's from a book. I read like crazy. Actually, I read the way a busy hooker . . . well, you know."

"May I ask what in the world you're talking about?"

"I need your advice. Desperately. I mean, honest to your darlin old Jehovah, Rabbi."

"Really, Jelly, you're behaving like . . ."

"Three eleven Wood Street in South Mannerville, two blocks east . . ."

It was preposterous, of course. The girl was obviously ill—probably "turned on," as the kids in his own Temple Youth Group were starting to express it. And besides, what in all creation did *he* have to do with . . .

The house had been the kind so indigenous to the old residential sections of Mannerville and South Mannerville: a plain, white, kind of fundamentalist frame, with a wide-screened porch and unobtrusive shutters. The interior was plainer still, pure Southern Baptist; sparse, unidentifiably traditional furniture, thin well-worn rugs, a few vaguely religious prints, an inevitable, very realistic rendering of the Crucifixion, and of course GOD BLESS OUR HOME crocheted above the mantel.

Jo Ellen "Jelly" Johnson, in lavender lounging pajamas, had been not only out of sight but out of time.

"They'd *kill* me if they knew I'd even thought about this outfit, much less actually *wore* it," she'd said; purred breathlessly in her little-girl voice. Following it with almost no breath at all in her big-girl one—"I knew you'd come. I knew that no matter what impropriety you might feel you wouldn't turn away from someone that needs help. And I do need help. I'm pretty fucked up, you know."

And it had been that way all evening: The crazy chameleon and the reticent rabbi (her words—she had a thing for alliteration—not his; how could he have begun to unravel the reasons he was even there, much less—?)

"I have a drink for you. You *do* drink bourbon?"

"Well, yes, I . . ."

"You'll never know what I went through to sneak this in the house. Daddy's a teetotaler, you know. I mean, the *original* one. Lord! Would you like another drink?"

"I've hardly begun this one . . ."

"Do you really believe in God?"

"Jelly, really, what is it you . . . ?"

"Repeat after me. Shammy Isrell Addynoy Ellyhaynoo . . ."

"You have no idea what you're saying . . ."

"I want to know. Tell me."

"Tell you what?"

"What it means. Your Shammy Yis . . ."

"It's *Sh'ma Yisroel Adonoi Elohenu Adonoi Echod. Boruch Ato Adonoi . . .*"

"thelordourgodthelordisone."

"Then why did you ask, Jelly?"

"Because I'm a bitch."

"You don't mean that."

"Billygoat! I mean everything I say! Anyway, how different is it from what Daddy says? Hebrew or no Hebrew. Anyway, Jew things interest me right now. I'm troubled."

"Jelly, what is it you . . . ?"

"I hope this drink's kinder."

"Jelly, please. You said you were troubled. And in seeking help . . . if that *is* what you're seeking . . . you turned, with all deliberateness, to a man of religion. Now . . ."

"Shit! Religion's practically the whole nut, don't you know that? Say, that's good, isn't it? The nut of a nut. Anyway, Daddy and his goddern tub-thumpin's enough to blow anybody's mind. That is, anybody with even the remotest *kind* of mind. And I say unto you, brothers and sisters, the Day of Judgment is at hand, yea verily 'tis at hand. So listen, brothers and sisters, I mean all you miserable mothers, you got to take *His* hand, *His* hand! He's holdin it out to you, see it? Feel it? That sweet hand of Jesus . . ."

"How can *I* help you, Jelly?"

"Jesus!"

"I think it best I go. You need either a good doctor or a large audience, not a rabbi. Thank you for the drink, I . . ."

"No. No, please. Don't go. I need to talk to you. Honest. I need to . . . oh, I don't know. Hear things, I guess. See things. Think things. Dream things. And then get the fuck out of Mannerville and run bareass naked down some long beautiful street in some big beautiful city. . . . Hey! I want to show you somethin. Look, aren't they the grooviest things you ever seen? *Saw?*"

"What in the . . . ?"

"My dog Isabella of Spain just had them. Yesterday mornin, in fact. They're blind as bats of course. Like all newborn things. Like all . . ."

"Jelly, did you put something in this drink? I feel . . ."

". . . blind, blind. And you can only hope that when they do see they won't be in some dark ugly place with nobody there to hug them and love them and be true with them, really true with them. Tell them how it is, not how it was, not how . . ."

"Jeh . . . Jelly . . . What did you . . . what did you put in this drink? I think I'm . . . Jeh . . ."

". . . lord how his daddy done it and his daddy's daddy done it andhisdaddysdaddysdaddy . . ."

He had come awake in a long, slow dream, a many-colored collage of unfamiliar shapes; only by langorous degrees aware of a small bed, a small room; of himself and the pleasure of himself; of a physical sensation at once startlingly exciting and reassuringly warm. Until finally, fully conscious, aware not only of his nakedness but of something happening to him, something being done to him . . .

Of a strange softness moving him gently to hardness. Of . . .

"Oh my God!" he'd screamed—thought he'd screamed—as the image of baby puppies came into focus, the tiny creatures everywhere, anywhere; blindly, hungrily. Then from somewhere in the room Jelly's unrestrained laughter, the helpless giggle of a prankish child, and her nakedness covering his; wildly . . .

"Looks like the old ladies' dreamboat is in for a big trip tonight," she said, still nursing her drink.

Jacob looked about him. The Crescent Carousel was at capacity, with several people waiting at the entrance. For a moment, he stiffened. He thought he saw, among them, Ben and Leah Katz from B'nai Israel, but it was some other couple, obviously tourists. That scene, as Jelly would say, hadn't blasted him yet; but it would, he knew. Every night, for three months, he'd prepared himself for it.

"Yes, a large crowd," he said, turning back to the still-unfathomable smile across from him.

"How was your day?" he asked, reaching for her hand.

"Dreamy," she said, in her deepest uch voice, slowly seducing his fingers with her own. She worked in various shifts as a waitress at the Rue de la Pay on Bourbon, running in between to try her hand at water colors in Pirate's Alley. "Of course I *did* have somethin to get me through it all. You were sensational this mornin, Jack, really sensational. Do *exactly* the same thing tomorrow mornin, will you?"

He knew he was flushed, even in the dimness. "Jelly, don't you ever think of anything besides . . . ?"

"Your body? Christ no. I dig it, darlin, and you're absolutely stuck with it. Besides . . . Lord, it's cold in here. Did you work on the book today?"

"I made notes," he said.

"Notes," she laughed, half seriously, half derisively. "Billygoat! I mean did you *write* . . . ?"

"Jelly, please, this is no time to . . ."

She brought her hand back to her iceless drink. "It was a stupid letter your wife wrote," she said.

He could only bite his lip. "You've been through my things again," he said, his eyes small, hard.

"Of course. You practically leave me an engraved invitation the way you leave everything around. Anyway . . ."

"Jelly, you know you are not to touch my papers, not under any circumstances. That was the agreement, we . . ."

"Shit fire, Jack, we're a little past that, wouldn't you say?" Laughing softly, softly mimicking a voice she'd never heard. "Jacob, Jacob, how can you truly say 'Good-bye, God' without sayin 'Good-bye, life' . . . ?"

"There are times when I'd like to kill you," he said; softly, too.

Her hand again. "I'm out of sight, remember? And if

you can't remember that, at least remember what you done—*did*—last night . . . and this mornin . . ."

He died; several times.

"Time to shovel it, Reb." Joe Capella, short, was tall above them.

Jelly punched the little man playfully in his very round belly. "Make it a smashin set," she said. "Cream 'em out." Adding brokenly, just a little brokenly, "I love you, Jack. Shit, I love you."

Half-drunk, drunk, in the midst of chatter the crowd applauded. He played, sang, half sang—

If ever I would leave you . . .

CHAPTER SIX

Of all things with her, times with her, the most beautiful, most painful, most insane, was waking with her. Touching the day with her.

It wasn't just a stirring beside him, bringing him slowly awake. It was an explosion. Always the first to open her eyes, she didn't simply reach out to him, seduce him to consciousness. She hurled him to it, smashed him to it, and always with some new and inventive wile. One morning it might be an attack on his middle, a cobra's attack, practically squeezing the life out of him. The next, rolling like the ocean in his ear or majestically biting his behind.

Today it was a frontal assault. She was astride him, groin to groin, her lean body unrelentless in its pressure.

"Jelly, what the hell are you . . . ?"

He was awake.

"Do you have to take a leak first?" she whispered. "I already did."

"The word is urinate," he said, and she kissed him; hard.

"Jelly"—when he could get his breath—"don't you ever let up?"

She laughed. "Never. I won't let up till you shed every shibboleth of sexuation inhibition—how do you like *them* words?—that ever even . . ."

"I'd say there's precious little left to shed."

"Wanna bet?"

"Jelly. Jelly, you crazy girl . . ."

"Oh Jack. Jack Jack Jack Jack Jack . . ."

"Hush," he said. "Don't talk with your mouth full." But gently, very gently.

Afterward, watching her dress (God, how he loved watching her dress. It was like experiencing it all over again. The way she tugged at her panty hose, as though she were caressing her own flesh—roughly, hurriedly, but nonetheless passionately. The way she wriggled into her waitress's skirt and blouse, as though it were the act of love itself. The way she ran a comb through her now hip-length blonde hair; and this slowly, thoughtfully, as though it were the languor of afterlove). Afterward, watching her dress, feeling the weight, the wonder, of three short months.

Three long years.

Years.

Had it really begun then, the night of the blind puppies? The poor, sad, startling blind puppies? Were the man and the boy so separate? The boy. If he dreams without definition, where else to turn but to God? The man. If he still dreams without definition, where else to turn but to . . .

Away from God?

"It's a real motherfucker."

"Jelly, I wish you wouldn't. That kind of affectation . . ."

"Affectation my ass. You have to learn to distinguish the natural from the unnatural, darlin. Now what was I talkin about?"

"Life."

"Yeah. Anyway, like I was sayin, it's a real . . ."

"I heard you."

Had he meant to see her again? He thought not. Been certain not. He'd never know. He had never been so repelled in his life. Or so drawn. The next week, weeks, endless Mannerville weeks, had been torture. She was a physical presence when he slept (if he slept at all), when he showered, shaved; sitting—alone, with a hundred rationales—dear God, he *had* been seduced!—and small redemption—in his temple study; standing in his pulpit, imprisoned, as it were, in the eyes of his congregation; in the living room, the kitchen, the bedroom, with Miriam; lying beside her, unable to touch her, frail bony Miriam, so sensitive to life, so insensibly without it. At least now. At least now in comparison. Now in . . .

He hated the disgusting *shikse!* He hated his own disgusting thoughts. He hated . . .

He had to see her again. If only to . . .

He needn't have worried.

"Hi. Feel like fuckin?"

She'd stood there, in the doorway, that half-derisive, half-teasing smile on her face; that face which somehow confronted, never just came upon you. He'd stood there, too, behind his desk—his own face, he was certain, like the frozen frame of a film.

"This happens to be a synagogue," he'd said. His voice, even in memory, exuded the smoke of dry ice.

And she'd laughed. "They say God forgives drunks and girls who've dropped a little acid."

"I see."

"No you don't. I just made it up. Anyway, how are you?"

"Well, thank you."

"Truthfully?"

"What is it you want, Jelly?"

"Ho-ho! The rabbi's big cock, what else?"

"I'm going to call your father."

"I'm not sure he has a cock. And if he does, and it ever stands up, I don't think it spews sperm. I think it recites the Lord's Prayer. Our father which art in heaven . . ."

"It seems almost a shame the Jews don't embrace the concept of the devil, Miss Johnson. You make it all so . . ."

"Real? Right. Now, let's go back to the word 'embrace.' I want you, you know. I think I might even be fallin in love with you. Uch! Sloppy, stupid . . ."

That night, in the shabby motel room on Highway 80 had been . . .

"Delicious. Just delicious. I feel like swallowin every ounce of sweat from every single pore of your body."

"Jelly, you're crazy, you're . . ."

"Yes. Oh Jack. Jack Jack Jack. Let's do it in the bathroom."

"The what?"

"The bathroom."

"You must be out of your mind."

"I am. You'll love it. Standin up, mid-air . . ."

"*My* mind! I'm out of *my* mind!"

"It's great when you're doin it the second time. Kind of earthy and real. Like . . ."

"You impossible child."

"A cunt, you mean. A real cunt. Oh God, I wish there

was a god, so I could tell him how much I love you, how . . ."

"Try and write today, darlin. You need it. You're real uptight. It's good to get the sweat off the balls, I always say. Maybe you oughta sing 'Jesus Christ, Superstar' to-night, just to shake yourself up."

"Have a good day, Jelly," he said.

"Depends on how well I feel like relatin to fags and dykes. You know the Rue de la Pay. New Orlin's purest dairy creamery. I love you, you know, Jack. I honest to shit do."

He lay there awhile, not really wanting to get up; not wanting to leave the smell of her, still so impudently alive on the sheets, the pillows. But the room in focus (in day-light maddening: the brass bed occupying at least three-quarters of it; battalions of skirts and blouses and stock-ings and bras, platoons of cosmetics, toiletries, flung like weary soldiers across the battlefield of a small dressing table, a single chair, which occupied the remaining fourth of it), the room in focus was against him. However hard he fought it, straightening up after her was a morning compulsion, even before coffee.

Instant coffee.

He smiled to himself, sipping it.

Would he ever get used to this crazy place, this "den of inequity in the bosom of St. Peter" as she called it? Prob-ably not, he thought. Even giving up a lifetime, how could you brush away a lifetime? *I'm sure you could eat rice puddin off Miriam Weiss's floor. Well, baby, mine have rice puddin on 'em!* Jelly.

Jelly.

He shook his head. It was true. Somehow rice pudding

was everywhere in the St. Peter Street apartment, in one way or another. You felt it in every crazy gypsy room. Just as you felt the impermanence, the transience, of the meager, characterless furnishings—what little you could see of them under the piled-up boxes, crates, dirty laundry, half-finished canvases, whatever. Four rooms, and they were all Jelly. Little of himself had become a presence. Except in a corner of the living room perhaps—that oddly charming high-ceilinged rectangle that, in spite of decades of indifference or abuse, had managed stubbornly to retain something of its Spanish aristocracy; a corner by narrow French doors that opened onto the balcony, a corner dominated by the oak desk from his seminary days, piled high with books and papers. From which he now, with set jaw, turned away.

It was a raw December day, particularly for New Orleans, but he walked out on the balcony anyway, a terry-cloth robe wrapped tight around him. Below, gray Rue de St. Peter was a rare mid-morning sparkler, cold sunlight embracing holly wreaths and papier-mâché stars and bright red candles, the quintessence of an almost old-fashioned Creole Christmas. It was actually cheerful.

"Better watch out, better not cry, better be good I'm a' tellin you why, Santa Claus is a'comin . . . !"

Jacob glanced down the balcony, to the open French doors of the next apartment, where Shy Thompson in an old T-shirt and Levi's stood in all his muscular glory. Not more than twenty-three, twenty-four, Shy was the come-on man for Sho-Girl Palace on Bourbon Street, probably the most ebullient barker in the Quarter, certainly the most successful outside attraction to women and men alike. Particularly certain specimens of the latter. Even in dead of winter Shy wore as little as possible, his constantly flexing, oversized arm muscles keeping him—as he put it —"warm as hogshit." Shy was a farm boy from Chopatoula Parish, who regarded himself as the bisexual miracle of the age. "*Tri-seckshul* ackshully," he sometimes modestly corrected. "I ain't above a possum or a sheep now'n then. 'Course *they's* got to be female, make no mistake about *that!*" Meanwhile, he shared one of the other third-floor apartments with an aging homosexual named Andrew P. Gatesworth, who owned one of the Quarter antique shops and "who I lets bugger me once in awhile, to keep his old spirits up." Shy (his real name was Hugo, which few knew, much less divulged) had befriended Jelly ever since she'd arrived in New Orleans. It was impossible not to like him.

". . . to town!" Jacob sang back, acknowledging him with a flourish of both arms.

A real belly laugh assaulted him. "You slay me, Jack, you really do, man. Whyncha do it with that smash endin at the old folks home t'night?"

Jacob smiled. "I might, Shy," he said. "I just might."

Shy joined him at the railing. "Dern," he said, squeezing his great arms. "Colder'n I figgered."

"Very," said Jacob.

"Feels good though. Feels real old good. Speshly after that inferno I been through. Whooee!! I let old Andy git to me this mawnin. I swear that old sweetie pie nearabout . . ."

Jacob looked away.

"You oughta let him do you sometime, Jack. I mean, no shit. I mean, humpin's great, hell I done it twice last night with one o' the straights at the Sho-Girl. An' I reckon there ain't no one I know of likes gettin his pipes cleaned by a chick better'n me, man. But you ain't quite lived till you got yerself done by a real cravin, God-fearin . . ."

Jacob stiffened, visibly, but said nothing.

Shy laughed. "I know, man, I know. Change the subject. Anyways, I was just testin you."

"Testing me?" said Jacob, turning quizzically back at him.

"In a way, yeah," said Shy, his voice still expansive but suddenly serious. "Guys like me, we might not've had much edjacation, an' what we broke out from might not seem like much to somebody broke off from the ministry, or whatever Jew folks call it. But guys like me—chicks like Jelly too—we don't screw around with our truth eternal. We live it up, down an' sideways. Once we found it, I mean."

"Your . . . truth eternal?" said Jacob, looking curiously, and not without interest, at the young, ruddy, dumb, not-so-dumb face beside him.

"Far as I'm concerned," said Shy. "Yeah. There's not one of us knows what it's all about, or what *we're* all about, or even if it's all about anything. So guys like me, we take our truth eternal where it's at, where it's *now*, an' we do an' say what's nachral to us. Leastways what feels an' sounds nachral to us. You can't shit that."

Jacob smiled, thought he smiled. "No," he said, "you can't . . . fault that."

Shy was quickly solicitous, almost gentle. "Hell, Jack, I didn' mean no offense. You're a good cat, man. I like you. It's just that sometimes you're still a little . . ."

"Uptight?" said Jacob. "Jelly's favorite word. One of them anyway."

"Yeah," said Shy, "I reckon. I reckon that's good a scripshun as any."

"I see. And what do you recommend, Shy?"

Who grinned broadly. "Hell, man, I told you. Pop in one mawnin an' let old Andy spring the joint."

The wind, from the corner at Royal, was suddenly, blessedly sharp. Jacob turned toward the French doors. "Have a good day, Shy," he said.

"Yeah. Yeah, you too," said Shy, turning—somewhat dispiritedly, shivering a little—toward his own open doors. "Git some good writin done, man. Good . . . good day fer it."

The warmth inside was not warming. Jacob lit a cigarette, by rote lingering in his small corner of the room that screamed her; thinking, not thinking, chilled and solemn. Knowing what he had to tackle, what he had to . . .

Was it chance alone that when he sat at the desk and opened the journal nearest him, that Miriam's letter (*My dear Jacob, I received the check and I suppose it is incumbent upon me to say Thank you although to understand this, to comprehend this, is still beyond*—in that incongruously large and swirling hand) should be folded into the page that bore that questioning entry, scrawled on that lost, miserable night in Mannerville, that night he had drunk too much, loved too much?

March 7.

Why? Why? Dear God, why? At a time in my life when it's all I can do just to go on with a life's work I've come more and more to feel some strange ambiguity toward, some perverse uninvolvement with, to find myself involved with a girl who not only stirs all the body juices so long suppressed but all the . . .

Chance alone?

"Jelly, this is the last time I'm going to see you, and there's no need even . . ."

"My tits are too small."

"What?"

"My tits are too small. I massage 'em all the time but nothin happens. Thank heaven I got good hips and a nice ass. Lay back down, Jack. You know you're not leavin. We got a thing and that's it. Besides. What girl in her right mind would let a hard-on like that get away?"

It was only the third time he'd been with her. It had seemed like the hundredth. It was a cold January night, one of the coldest in North Louisiana's memory. They were in a motel room in Bossier City, just outside Shreveport. He had told Miriam he would be in Shreveport for the night to discuss a joint Youth Group seminar between two Shreveport congregations and Mannerville's. And indeed he had met with the other rabbis earlier in the evening. But deception was still heavy with him as he mounted her again, even if it dimmed with the rest of the world when he was safe inside her. *Surely God is at the zenith of the heavens and looks down on all the stars, high as they are. But you say, "What does God know? Can he see through thick darkness to judge? His eyes cannot pierce the curtain of the clouds . . ."*

Rabbi. Rabbi Jacob Weiss. Scholar, he thought ruefully. Good rabbinical scholar. Good rab . . .

"Jack, harder, harder, tear up my guts, my brain . . ."

"Don't talk, don't . . ."

"Oh Jesus, Jesus . . ."

"Yes . . ."

"Jesus. For Daddy. Pound it home for Daddy . . ."

"You're crazy . . ."

"Crazy. Crazy Crazy Crazy I'll die, I think I'm going to die. Oh, you man, you beautiful man. I wish I could get all of you in me, your ass, your legs, your . . . Jack! Jack, oh lord, oh darlin, yes, yes! I'll die, I'll . . ."

In wetness, exhausted, her face almost a part of his underarm, his in some far place (her sweat-sweet hair, neck?) he had known he couldn't leave, known he would stay the night; the night at least.

And somewhere in it:

"You really dig me, don't you? I mean, you really do."

"Wha . . . ?"

"Don't pretend you're asleep. Your leg's been nibblin at mine like a catfish for an hour. A good hour."

"Jelly, please. I have to sleep. Tomorrow's an incredible day. I have to meet with the temple board, I have the Youth Group committee coming in, I have Friday night's sermon to . . ."

"Jack? How did you become a rabbi?"

"Just luck I guess."

"You *do* have a sense of humor. Oh I could eat you up!"

"Jelly, don't, you know I . . ."

"Lord, what a protester! I wish you'd put some of that energy to protestin somethin bad, not somethin good like this . . . and this . . . and this . . ."

"Jelly . . ."

"Jack. Jack Jack Jack. I was serious, you know. About what made you become a rabbi."

"I know you were. But I can't honestly answer you. I suppose because . . . Jelly, I really don't want to talk about it."

"You're ashamed, that's why. Of what you're doin here, I mean. It don't—*doesn't*—matter how much crap old Almighty makes you take, if you do one sweet pleasurable thing you got to call it sin. I guess Jew preachers don't really differ much from Baptist ones."

"Jelly, don't use that expression again. Ever. Please."

"What expression? Jew preacher? Okay. That's a small favor to grant somebody who gives so much . . . so . . . Jack?"

"Mmn?"

"What were you like as a boy?"

"I don't know. Bookish, I suppose."

"I know. I mean, I guessed. And would you believe somethin? So was I. I mean, I couldn't get enough of books, ever. I still read a lot. I bet you didn't know that. I just finished readin a book by Kafka. Because he was Jewish I guess. Because of you. Does that surprise you?"

"I don't think anything about you would surprise me."

"Wanna bet?"

"Oh God, you crazy girl . . ."

"Relax, Rabbi. I bet even the old Hebrew prophets knew that your so-called unclean meat was the tastiest."

And just before dawn, just after (too blinded by her to know?), she'd had an attack of the hiccups and started to giggle uncontrollably, and of course joyously attacked him again.

But just before they'd left the motel for the trip back to Mannerville, in their separate cars, he'd known what he had to do; say.

"I meant what I said last night, Jelly. Jo Ellen. We can't see each other again."

"Oh? My. I didn't realize rabbis recited soap-opera scripts too. Gee."

"Goddamnit, aren't you ever serious?"

"Wow! Listen to the man. I mean, how many commandments can you break in twenty-four hours? Now . . . I'll answer you. You're fuckin-A right I can be serious! Mister, I've never been so serious in my life. I'm so screwed up in love with you it's a wonder my brain hasn't blowed. *Blown!*"

"Jelly, don't. There's no need to get yourself all . . ."

"Jack, I love you. I'm nineteen years old, twenty in three months, I'm in my second year at Northeast State, which I could throw up from, I'm warm, I'm givin, I'm pretty way out, I'm really mad as a hatter, but I'm not a hippie or whatever you'd like to think, even if I do smoke grass once in awhile, I'm a woman, Jack, so much a woman inside me I could scream sometimes, I was laid by exactly three boys before I met you and I acted smart and generous and brave and raunchy and got a quick reputation which I'm just perverse enough to enjoy and they didn't mean a thing, nothin, except maybe Bobby T., he was a tough screw, but you're my first man, I mean my first real *man*, I can't get enough of you and you know it, and you can't get enough of me and you know that too, even if you are a man of the cloth or whatever they call rabbis, and if you think the last two months was hell for you—*were* hell for you—well baby just wait for the next two . . ."

"Jelly, what are you trying to do to me?"

"Love you. Just love you. Jack, who am I in competition with? Your God? Your big hot-blooded God? Or is it her? *She*. Your friggin frigid . . ."

He slammed the journal shut, its sound not unlike that of his hand across her face—before he'd taken her—small, wounded, sobbing child—back into his arms.

He knew he wouldn't write; not this morning. (Or yesterday, or the day before?) In a kind of familiar resignation he pulled on Levi's and a turtle-neck sweater, slipped into an old Army-type fatigue jacket and, still unshaven, his hair uncombed, descended the two flights of stairs to the street.

Unlike the few minutes on the balcony, the wind's sharpness now was salve. It cut through weeks, months, years with the precision of an electric knife, leaving only the raw clear morning; noon. Gratefully, he breathed it in.

There was no decision as to where he would go. His direction, when he couldn't work—wouldn't—was always the same. Up Royal past the St. Louis Cathedral to St. Ann Street, the Presbytere Museum, one of the Pontalba buildings, the Old French Market (café au lait and a beignet at the Café du Monde; unemotionally, when possible), down Decatur Street past Jackson Square, the Cabildo, the other Pontalba—the tourist's route, but one he never tired of. Even on the chattiest morning (and chatter was as indigenous to the Vieux Carré as the Cabildo itself) there was an almost sepulchral quiet, the chatter itself a kind of choir.

On down Decatur to Iberville, across Chartres, Exchange Place, Royal, to Bourbon—and Jelly, Jelly's street. He did think of it as that. Passing the Rue de la Pay, he neither paused nor looked aside; he rarely did. He wasn't certain why.

Three doors up, at the Kool Kat, a rock group called the Kat's Klaws was imperturbably blasting the midday peace, while a few steps further, at the Old Absinthe House, a group of well-dressed, well-oiled businessmen were pouring forth "O Come All Ye Faithful" to the top of their lungs. It was in the air—the holidays, Christmas.

Hanukkah. Jacob had to smile, however wryly. Hanukkah too, he thought; Festival of Lights. It wasn't with lightning suddenness that he remembered that today (tonight) was the eve of Hanukkah. It had been with him since he'd come awake. Remote, hollow, a faraway song. It sang in his brain, all the way back to St. Peter, amid the red and green tinsel—the words rabbis and congregations would be reciting together like sheep, faithful vocal sheep, all across the country.

On this festival of Hanukkah we rededicate ourselves to Thee and Thy service. As we kindle the Hanukkah lights in our homes and our temples, may the light of Thy presence and Thy truth shine forth to dispel all darkness and lead all men unto Thee.

Amen.

CHAPTER SEVEN

. . . I've got the sun in the morning
And the moon at night . . .

It was a slow night, considering the season. Jacob knew his delivery was off as well. He had become too used to large audiences. Tonight's, at least for the second set, was almost studiedly scattered. And strangely laconic. As though anything more than a polite, perfunctory response would be a breach of etiquette, even break a law. But then again it probably wasn't they—them—at all. Simply he—him—too distant and preoccupied to find much emotion in, much less project.

. . . sun in the morning and the moon . . .

He didn't conclude the song exactly, he merely kept picking at the keyboard, segueing into "Dear Hearts and

Gentle People," sans lyrics. His mouth felt extraordinarily dry. He played by rote.

"Lousy night, Reb. Right? So? In my business you got to wing it, wing it all the way. There's good times, there's bad times, right? Only you ain't exactly no seducer of song tonight, fella. Got a bone on or somethin?"

Jacob didn't have to look up or around to know that Joe Capella was practically attached to his ear, delivering his casual confidences as though they were veiled Mafia threats.

"What is it you want to say, Joe?" he replied; fingers suddenly eager, even brilliant, on the keys.

"Nothin, Reb, nothin"—in the oily nasality that passed for a voice—"just assessin, that's all. Only it might not be a bad idea to throw in a jazz thing now and then. You know? Even a rock number once in awhile. What the hell. Barflies is barflies. And if honey don't get 'em you got to try a little molasses. A little *sassy* molasses if you know what I mean."

"Oh? And I thought it was my sex appeal that brought 'em in," Jacob said drily.

"Yeah, that's a good one, that's real cute, Reb. Don't read me wrong though. I ain't complainin. Off nights always get me itchy. Still, you got to be practical, you know? It's a lousy, dirty world out there, sweetheart. Nobody gives you nothin, right? You got a great voice, Reb. You got a great future in this business, no doubt about that. It's just that you got to loosen up more, get yourself a little more versatility. You know? Sooner or later the novelty wears off, even for singin ex-rabbis."

Without looking up or changing either pace or expression, Jacob said softly, even pleasantly, "Joe, why don't you stop waving your diploma from charm school and dissolve somewhere?" (Or as Jelly would put it, go . . .) Surprising, oddly delighting, himself. And uncertain of Capella's reaction, but in suddenly vigorous voice, threw himself into a resounding "Shenandoah." The room—he could physically feel it—came alive.

At the end of the set, smiling acknowledgment of the applause, he went to his usual back booth, and unusually, ordered a bourbon and soda. The waitress who brought it (Sally something. He could never remember. How much a part of, and apart from, the Crescent Carousel he still was) said casually, "There was a man here looking for you this afternoon, Jack. He said he'd come back tonight." Which he as casually dismissed; forgot. Already the small notebook secreted in the inside pocket of his tuxedo jacket was out of it, open in his hands, his scrawled notes of the afternoon safely before him.

"Hi."

"Hi."

Her hand covering his was strong, and very warm. Glancing up, he saw that Shy was with her.

Effusive as ever! "I come along in my cawfy break . . . good one, hunh? Cawfy break? . . . to learn if old hearts and old crotches keep time together."

"Keep what?" said Jacob.

"Time together. You know. With the beat."

"Oh."

Jelly half laughed, easing in beside him. "Billygoat! I just happened to pass by the Sho-Girl and he just happened to be at loose ends for a half hour and with all the queens, dykes, and silly horny straights that was—*were*—positively crazy to be chummy with me today I invited him along. To protect me from that lecherous old doorman at the Royal Sonesta. Not to mention the two hours I pissed away on that silly watercolor of the nympho climbin a pillar of the Cabildo."

"I see you're on one tonight," said Jacob. Shy, with his wide grin, sat across from them.

"Not really," she said. "It's just such a relief to see you I guess. I reckon. I reckon." Touching his hand again; the papers. Slipping them back into his jacket, he felt strangely (no, not so strangely) like a traitor.

"What's that?" Shy asked, sham innocence no stranger to his handsome face. "Some more of your secret porno?"

"You *could* call it that," said Jelly. But with a quiet, almost timid, gentleness. "It's the Holy Writ, Shy. Even the sweetest pussy in the world is no substitute for God, Shy. *Or* guilt. Guilt, the darlin, the good companion . . ."

". . . The one emotion you can count on when all the rest desert you. Lordy, Lordy, how could we survive without it? As Daddy would say, 'The mo' burdensome yo' sin, the nearer you gettin to Salvation!' "

"Jelly, please I'm . . . it's rough enough without . . ."

And it was; had been. Balancing his two lives (and he *had* come to see them as that; in Mannerville, live them as that) was not unlike the balancing of two conflicting ideologies, or two diametrically opposing views from the same tongue, on the same issue, as in the Talmud. In dreams, nightmares—flying, being flown, like a badminton bird, over a net of confusion, a net of unresolve; taut, fragile net; threatening string. A boy's passion (What else? Had he ever really known it before?) on one side, a man's duty, responsibility (and *damn* the words, the thought; so inescapable, both) on the other. Imprisoned for the first time in his life on a seemingly isolated course, rationalizing every play, every set, the whole ludicrous, endless game. Waking—in Jelly's bed; Miriam's; irrevocably, his own—to perspire for hours on end, sleep again as elusive as the Promised Land; wakefulness—even in hell—perhaps the blessing. Only, finally, in darkness or dawn, to creep from bedroom to bathroom to vomit at least the presence of it—of himself!—up.

"What's happening to you, Jacob? You're not well, I can see it. I'm going to call Dr. Snyder . . ."—Miriam all quiet concern, quiet childless mother.

"If you'd stop this silly dramatizin which I must say, Jack darlin, is takin you on a real nowhere trip . . ."—Jelly all child, all woman-child, all . . .

February 25.

We speak, in our litany, of His wisdom, His strength. Do we not? Do I not? "Infinite as is Thy power even so is Thy love. Thou didst manifest it through Israel Thy people. By laws and commandments, by statutes and ordinances hast Thou led us in the way of righteousness and brought us to the light of truth. Therefore at our lying down and our rising up, we will meditate on Thy teachings and find in Thy laws true life and length of days. O That Thy love may never depart from our hearts. Praised be Thou, O Lord . . ."

March 3.

. . . be merciful to us in our failings and trespasses and, when we have gone astray, help us to find our way back to Thee. Grant us vision and courage, that, unhindered and unafraid, we may pursue the paths of truth and duty. Enlighten our minds . . . Dear God, Jelly was there in a rear pew . . . !

March 4.

Are we ever the child, His wrongdoing child? Bowing the head and bending the knee . . . ?

March 11.

Thou, O Lord, hast endowed us with reason to distinguish between right and wrong and with freedom to choose between good and evil. Though Thy greatness is beyond our understanding, Thou art near to the hearts of the lowly who seek Thee and who strive to do Thy will. Teach us to be firm . . ." Jelly there in the back pew again? Again?

March 12.

Vohavto ays Adonoi elohechu b-chol l'vovcho uvchol . . . *and Jelly, Jelly, it's you who are right, you who . . .*

He had taken to seeing her days; afternoons. Which in Mannerville was tantamount to the death wish. Usually it was on Mondays and Wednesdays, when she had no afternoon classes and he could get away for several hours, even under the quizzical gaze of Bertha Gratz, the temple's spinster secretary, for whom he always had some vague suggestion of going downtown to visit with one or more of the member merchants or making hospital rounds or dropping in at the parish library.

They met at motels outside the city limits, sometimes between Mannerville and Ruston, sometimes between Mannerville and Tallulah, occasionally as far as the outskirts of Vicksburg. The whole incredible affair tearing him inside out—until he was inside the always antiseptic room and she was in his arms.

Or he hers.

"For a minute I thought you weren't comin. I almost died."

"Don't think *not* coming doesn't enter my mind a hundred times a day. But here I am."

"Because you love me. Say it. Say it's because you love me."

"I don't know what it is. I don't know what's happening to me, what . . ."

"Don't. It's all right. I don't care if you're just a horny old rabbi, as long as you're here, as long as I can see you, touch you, smell you . . ."

"English Lit must have been excruciating today. Chaucer?"

"Who cares? A bitch in heat is a bitch in heat, no matter how you slice it. And slicin it's what you're here for, Jack . . . slicin it, darlin, slicin it . . ."

"Jesus . . . Jesus . . ."

"Ho-ho. The rabbi made a no-no. Say it again."

"Jelly . . ."

"Silly. You know what I mean. *Jesus.* The way you say it. Say it again."

"Jelly, what are you trying to . . . ?"

"Say it."

". . . Jesus . . ."

"Yes. Like a man with a woman. Again. Again."

". . . Jesus . . ."

"Yes. Not like Daddy. Not pathetic, sanctimonious, like . . . like Daddy . . ."

Daddy came to his temple study one late March day, ironically as his daughter had: unannounced. He was not an unimpressive figure in his black suit, black tie—redneck, country boy, these never fully to be scrubbed from his flesh, but with something of authority, even dignity, all the same. Mostly, however, with a look and a walk that Jelly called his "portly piety."

"Rabbi Weese?"

His voice, unmistakably, had the preacher's timber.

"Weiss," he'd corrected softly; standing.

And to the manner born: "I presume, suh, I am not interruptin?"

"No. Please . . ." Proffering the chair across from him.

"I don't believe we've formally met, Rabbi, although I have seen you, suh, at a Mannerville Council of Churches meetin or two. I am the Reverend Josephus Johnson of the First Baptist Church of South Mannerville."

"Yes, I know."

"I come on a most distressin errand, Rabbi, a most distressin errand."

"Oh?"

"One that as a servant of the Lard—as you, suh, as you —I find perhaps not to the likin of the Lard, but for His sake, Rabbi, for His sake."

"I see." On guard, wondering: Can he possibly have any inkling . . . ?

"It's my daughter Jo Ellen, Rabbi."

Oh God . . .

"Strange child. Strange strange child. She has long been our cross, my good wife Beulah's and mine. Long, long. Even with the good Lard Himself residin in the house she was raised in she has, alas, defied Him, defiled Him, de—" (The pause: significant?) "*Our* Lard, I mean, Rabbi. *Our* Lard who gave His only begotten Son . . ."

He had relaxed, somehow. "How may I be of help to you, Reverend? I must tell you right off that I'm not quite up to . . . theological differences and complexities . . . this morning. But aside from that I am at your service."

"I thank you, suh, I thank you. Now . . . as to why I am here . . ."

"Yes, Reverend?"

"It is my understandin, Rabbi, that my daughter Jo Ellen—strange child, strange—that my daughter Jo Ellen has not only been attendin your . . . Friday evenin services? . . . but attendin your counsel as well."

"My counsel?"

Would he never get to the . . . ?

"Rabbi Wise. Suh. Is Jo Ellen contemplatin . . . Jewism?"

He'd done his best not to smile. "Do you mean is your daughter inclined spiritually—even intellectually—toward Judaism? I . . . I would hardly know that, Reverend. She *has* come to the synagogue—temple—several times. Often with a friend of hers, I believe—Shirley Goldstein—the daughter of a member of Congregation Isaiah. And she *has* asked me several questions, that is, concerning our faith. Aside from that, I have observed nothing that would indicate more than . . . more than academic interest. I can tell you little else, Reverend Johnson. I know little else."

And I won't sleep well tonight, he thought. I won't sleep at all well tonight.

"I want no misunderstandin, Rabbi. No misunderstandin whatsoever. Whatsoever. Just reassurin, suh, reassurin. I'm a true believer, Rabbi, in the brotherhood of man, under the good Lard Almighty, no matter what our . . . our differences."

Softly. Wryly? "I doubt very much, Reverend, that your daughter—Jo Ellen?—that she has any inclination, much less intention, of embracing the Jewish faith."

Later, mentioning it to Jelly only that she stop coming

to Friday night services so often, to his office so often . . .

"Shit! Or *shee-utt* as he would say if the hypocritical bastard ever let himself go. I'm my own bein, Jack, it don't —*doesn't*—matter what he or anybody . . . You're disturbed. Darlin, I know it, you are, you're disturbed. And I love you so, I do. I love you so much I . . . *Fuck him!* Fuck all of 'em! It's you and me, Jack—all right, you and *I*. It's all that . . . Billygoat! Billygoat! I guess next you'll be gettin an engraved callin card from your wife . . ."

"My wife? Now what's *that* supposed to mean?"

"Oh nothin. Nothin at all . . ."

(Miriam! Could she possibly know? Miriam—whom he could hardly touch now, who . . . Miriam! Whose body now was like his own, a thing to be endured, not comforted by. Miriam! Whose eyes suddenly were too dull, whose nostrils were too wide, whose . . . Awkward and graceless in her old-fashioned nightgown, barren and abrasive in her logic, her . . . Miriam! Surely she couldn't suspect the remotest . . .)

"I don't know what you're hinting at, Jelly, but if my wife's in any way implicated, I swear to God . . ."

"God! God! Where it all begins. All the stupid burden, the lousy guilt . . ."

". . . what it all boils down to, Shy. God the father, the holy . . ."

There were a few more couples in the Carousel now, several more singles. Voices, a kind of ambient intrusion, sounded nervously expectant.

"I don't know what you're talkin 'bout half the time, Jel," said Shy, sliding from the booth, "but I love you anyways. You're a cool cat, too, Jack. Now I got to get my ass back to the voyagers."

"The what?" said Jacob.

"The voyagers. You know. The cats who get their rocks off lookin 'stead of doin. Voyagers. Right?"

"If you say so, Shy," said Jelly.

"Peace," said Shy.

In the stereo coin machine at the entrance Barbra Streisand was midway through "Second-Hand Rose." Jacob sipped at his drink, in silence. Jelly was suddenly silent too. For some reason it seemed a time for silence. When Engelbert Humperdinck began the concluding lyric of "The Way It Used To Be" Jacob said, "Back to dreamland" and Jelly said, "Peace."

Several requests confronted him as he climbed back on the revolving bar.

" 'Autumn Leaves,' Jack."

" 'Galveston,' Jack."

" 'Dream a Little Dream of . . .' "

He smiled thoughtfully—he thought—and began playing and singing, convivially,

Way down yonder in New Orleans

looking absently about him. He was no more than a quarter of the way into it when he saw his brother Sam and his wife Esther, from Dallas, standing solemnly in the room's center. And though his heart skipped a beat, his voice and fingers didn't. He was, after all, Jack White, performer, professional; sorcerer of song.

CHAPTER EIGHT

Song, talk; above all, laughter. They laugh very seriously in the Quarter in New Orleans.

Very seriously.

Way down yonder in . . .

"You both look well," said Jacob. "I suppose I have no reason to think otherwise."

They were in the Rib Room of the Royal Orleans Hotel, an elegant, almost make-believe oasis after the desert of shrieking sands along the five short blocks they'd walked —in uncomfortable silence.

"We're well," said Sam Weiss. Not unlike Jacob in the way he said it; the way he looked as he said it. He hadn't the clear good looks of Jacob, he was heavier and his hair was graying, thinning, he was coarser even; but his gestures, particularly the way he used his hands palm down, rarely up, and the way he held his head, rather pridefully, erect, were very familial.

"And Papa?" said Jacob.

"Papa's well too," said his brother. "He still hasn't the use of his left arm. But on the whole, well."

"The children? Hannah and Myron?"

"Well, Jacob. Yes. well."

The stiffness, the strangeness, were stifling. And it was very warm in the posh, holiday-festive room. The fragrance of charcoal beef was somehow too heavy, too pervading.

"I suppose it's gratuitous to ask after the business?" he said.

"The business is fine," said Sam Weiss. "Not prosperous-prosperous but . . . prosperous. Yes. Everything and everybody are . . . well."

"In both body *and* mind," said Esther Weiss, a large—that is, broad—but not unpretty woman in her late thirties. She had rather thick features but on such an expanse of face and with expensive makeup they had the distinction of belonging. Her upswept hair, obviously only hours from a beauty parlor, was coal black and her eyes (deep and Semitic, the loveliest part of her) were dark as well. "Yes. Well in both body *and* mind. Which is more than we can say for *some* people."

"Esther, please . . ." Sam Weiss's voice, while low, was deep with authority.

Jacob looked about him, at the well-dressed patrons, the well-appointed tables, the quiet Christmas decorations, his eyes moving from one to another without seeing any of them. Only reluctantly did he bring himself back to his own table. He was certain that his brother and sister-in-law had played the same uneasy game. Without letting himself reflect on it, Jacob knew that this was a moment destined, one he had perhaps dreaded the most. He felt as genuinely sorry for their obvious discomfort as he felt acutely conscious of his own.

But his voice was even and conversationally pitched when he spoke again: "Sam. Esther. Why don't we just bring it out into the open? I know you didn't leave the business at this time of the year to come sight-seeing in New Orleans."

It was Esther Weiss whose sigh was audible. "How could you? How *could* you? A rabbi, a scholar, a . . . I could have died in that place tonight when I heard you singing. I tell you, I could have *died*. And don't think Sam and I don't know about that girl. Don't think we didn't manage to find out. You can just thank God we've been able to keep it from Papa. Kill him, that's what it would do, kill him. A knife in his heart, that's what it would be, a knife in his poor dear . . ."

"Esther!" Her husband's tone was unmistakable. "I'll do the talking, if you don't mind."

His wife's face was frozen in anger and resentment but she kept her peace.

"You sang great," he said, turning to him full-face. "You always did have a fine voice. Even when you were no higher than . . ."

"Thank you," said Jacob. He knew that the anguish on his brother's face was real. Uncertainly, he managed a vague smile to camouflage his own.

"Like a sweet bird, Mama used to say. Or was it a bird in heaven? It's hard to remember, it seems so long . . . I wrote you four times, Jacob. Four times. The way you said, by General Delivery, when you wrote you were . . . Four *verkochter* times!"

"I know. I read all of them with deep respect, Sam. All of them."

"Respect, Jacob? I see. Respect enough to read them but not respect enough to pick up a fountain pen and . . ."

"I couldn't. I'm sorry. I simply couldn't."

"Oh?" Esther—her husband for once be damned—interjected. "You got arthritis in your hand too? Not just your head?"

Ignoring her, Sam Weiss said, "A line or two, Jacob. That's all. A line or two. You could have been dead, all we knew."

"That's not true, Sam," Jacob said softly. "I knew you were in touch with Clifford Weinberg at the temple. He called me."

Sam Weiss looked down at his folded hands. His eyes were brothers to the room's dim lights. "I always thought I understood you," he said. "I have to come to middle age to find out I don't understand you at all."

"No one has to understand another, Sam. Just accept them."

His brother lifted his eyes slowly. "Why have you done all this, Jacob?" he asked. Jacob was certain there were tears in his voice.

"I really don't want to talk about it, Sam," he said. "Times change, people change, I . . . I don't want to talk about it, Sam."

"Would you prefer talking about *her?*" Esther hissed, or so it sounded, through a mouthful of Caesar salad.

Again her husband ignored her, although the knuckles of his folded hands—Jacob could see—were taut and white. "How you wanted to be a rabbi," he said. "I never saw such a devotion, such a . . . You made us all proud, proud to be Jews, proud to be . . . Was that her back there? The girl in the booth?". .

"Yes," he said. "That was Jelly."

"*Jelly!*" Now the hiss in Esther's voice was unmistakable.

"Does she mean that much to you, this girl, this *shikse?*" asked Sam Weiss.

"She means a very great deal to me," said Jacob.

Sam Weiss's eyes narrowed, the lines about his mouth deepened. "Then it's going to be that much harder saying good-bye," he said. Pausing almost dramatically, which for so undramatic a man was chilling. "We've heard from Miriam, Jacob. She didn't know what to do, how to tell you. She's pregnant."

The prime ribs were thick, rare, incredibly tender, but Jacob didn't remember touching them.

A light rain was falling as he made his way back to the Carousel. But the thick crowds on the narrow sidewalks were not deterred by it. Mostly they were young, members of the Quarter's not inconsiderable hippie community, and several greeted him when he passed. A boy with long gold hair, wearing a dirty white bathrobe, called out volubly, cheerfully, "Hail, Ex!" Although Jacob performed in one of the "squarest" of the "street people" establishments, his status as a "rabbi who kicked it" rendered him respect rarely given a "straight."

(And communication. "Hey, Ex! If they defrock a priest, what do they do with a rabbi?")

Tonight, however, his own response was unspoken. But inside him, loud, so *goddamn* loud . . .

If anyone has committed a serious sin, let him beware of thinking of it, for where our thoughts are, there we also are with our soul. Let not your soul sink . . .

Jelly had left the Carousel and he played and sang his remaining sets of the evening with only perfunctory style, drinking heavily between. When he arrived back at the apartment at three—the rain heavier now, emotional—he was slightly drunk.

She was still awake, as he'd known she would be, sitting cross-legged in the middle of the bed in her tiny thigh-length blue nightdress and her big Granny glasses, reading, pretending to read, a paperback of *Catch 22.*

"Jack? What the fuck . . . ?"—And it was all she got to say, because he literally tore his clothes from his body and took her as he had never taken her before: roughly, his mouth the producer of a thousand tongues, his groin the inventor of a thousand miracles. On the bed, the floor, entangled in sheets, dirty laundry. In the bathroom, the living room, the kitchen. Among unfinished canvases, long-finished food. Among books, the pages of books. Buber, Babel, Thomas Aquinas, Santayana, Spinoza. Erich Fromm, Goethe. Maimonides. The Talmud. Confounding her, confusing her, commemorating her—remembering her. Cementing her in animal mastery, mystery, to every contour of his body, his mind.

She responded naturally, with great passion and great joy, and never knew, he was certain, that his wild crazy laughter wasn't laughter at all.

Part Three

✲ ✲ ✲ ✲ ✲ ✲ ✲ ✲

CHAPTER NINE

"More duck, Jacob?"

"No, thank you."

"Peas? I've plenty peas."

"No, I'm fine."

"You hardly eat."

"I'm not very hungry."

"You used to adore food."

"I suppose, yes."

"It's that place. The hours."

"I think I'll lie down."

"I have dessert."

"Later perhaps."

"That wonderful *liebekuchen* from Katz's. You know how you . . ."

"Later."

"The baby."

"What?"

"The baby. It moved."

"Yes. It won't be long."

"No. Not long. Not long at all."

"I'll just rest a few minutes."

"There's a letter from Esther on your desk."

"I'll read it later."

"Your father's ailing again."

"Oh? I'm sorry."

"They want us in Dallas. Sam wants you in the business."

"I've told you. I have no intention of going in the business."

"It's Sam asking, Jacob. Not I. Coffee?"

"Later."

"Yes. Later. Later later later later. I know you don't love me, Jacob. I knew that when I came back. But you don't even like me. You don't like me at all. But please, Jacob. A small piece of cake, you need your strength. All those drinks you had before we ate. The wine. They have to be absorbed by something solid, something . . ."

"To hell with your cake!"

"I . . . I'm sorry."

"Yes, so am I. I just want to lie down."

"Of course. Poor Jacob. My poor dear Jacob."

"Oh for God's sake, Miriam . . ."

She had returned to New Orleans in January, one of the coldest Januarys on record, the wind whipping and snapping across the entire Gulf Coast for days on end, with no end in sight. It was not the most agreeable time for resettling.

He had rented a small house in the Metarie district, a considerable distance from the Quarter. He had kept his job at the Crescent Carousel, although it weighed upon them, between them—him and Miriam—like chronic indigestion. She stayed home almost every night, except for an occasional visit with a friend she had made, a Selma Feinberg, down the block, and Fridays when she attended services at a Conservative synagogue on Tulane Avenue. So much for the nights. Days, they had their main meal in mid-afternoon (she kosher still; he trying consciously neither to notice nor be encumbered by it) and he spent the few hours before and after trying to sort out the few papers left him, as Jelly had destroyed the bulk of them the morning he'd left her.

The morning she'd . . .

("Baby? A baby? You can flush the baby down the friggin toilet for all I care! Oh brother! Brother John and Luke and Matthew and Jeremiah! So what else is new? Billygoat! Same old guilt, same old shit. Values! Lordy me. You call what you're doin Values? You call all those high-minded Jew principles that reject life in favor of livin death—yes, livin death!—Values? Well, shit fire, as they say where I come from. I'll tell you what Values are, Rabbi. Values are this!"—tearing her minigown from her body as though it were no more than a bothersome thread; standing there among the careless accumulations of the most intoxicating weeks of his life in her nakedness, her shameless pride, every treasured part of her pink with anger, livid with hurt—"this and this and all that goes with 'em, Buster Brown! Not decency, not morality . . . but not decadence either, baby. Because that's what you're going back to. Decadence, disease, despicableness, de—" in childlike uncertainty searching about the room, so alone, so vulnerable; suddenly—violently—pulling books, notebooks, papers from his desk, rushing with them in her crazed nakedness to the terrace where she tore them into shreds, feeding them to the hungry river winds; crying back to him almost insensibly over her beautiful bare shoulder—"*That* for your Jew God! *That* for your Jew book! *That* for your . . ."—he paralyzed, helpless, unable even to call her in from the cruel December air. Unable . . .)

It was April now, one of the more gracious months in New Orleans. The breezes from the Mississippi were as pleasant as love taps, carrying with them the sweetness of hydrangea and azalea and oleander and magnolia—old friends in an orgy of scent. The air itself, while light with relief from its burden of winter, was heavy with the promise of summer.

And Miriam was heavy with child.

Jacob couldn't bear to look at her, not directly at her, especially when she was sitting—the oval-shaped swelling like a clothed goiter in her lap (she was carrying low, small), the thing she'd so wanted, the thing of him.

He.

Be fruitful, and multiply, and replenish the earth.

(And always at the edge of thought: It *had* to be a night just before the High Holidays, the night she'd been so restless, he so frustrated by indecision; passionless, yes; clumsy, yes; still . . .)

They slept apart; had since she'd returned. Unspoken between them, it was now a life style for them. Nor did they look upon each other unclothed. (Not that they ever had. Even in the first days of their union she had not permitted, much less invited, the sight of her. Nor allowed herself, in quiet submission, the sight of him.) In many ways it was a monastic life.

("When you hanker for a hunk of real ass, darlin . . .

and you will"—Jelly's last words in parting, soft, with great dignity—"jerk off!")

He drank a great deal. Something he had never done before. And dreamed. He had never dreamed, or at least remembered dreaming, so profusely; so recurringly. (A corridor, yes. A hospital corridor. A delivery room. No. A sanctuary. "Your baby, Rabbi, your baby. A fine, healthy boy-child, man-child, man, god-child, god . . ." Taking it, holding it, all eighteen pounds of it, gently carved posts, the finest silk, mewling puking scrolls of the arc. *Sh'ma Yisroel Adonai Elohenu . . .*)

The nights were long, the days longer. At the Crescent Carousel he added islands of Simon and Garfunkel, The Beatles (past), Janis Joplin, The Rolling Stones, and Sly and The Family Stone to his repertoire; business picked up. In his study at the house (Study? The dining-room table, once cleared) he drafted new notes (not text; not yet)—a peripatetic (and largely futile) exercise in which *God and Guilt: The Inseparables* was re-cast into *The Jew Without God: Is It Possible?*, an inquiry into the perpetuation of the Jewish mystique without the Oneness that had given it both its tradition and its staying power; not in the theological or metaphysical sense, not as a transcendental or incorporeal tract, but as a social, even moral, phenomenon; e.g., Is the morality of the Jew totally dependent upon a belief in God or can the Jew, the contemporary Jew, maintain his thousands of years' inheritance—*as a Jew*—in a world and a time where divinity, and father-figure inspiration, must somehow—and by some moral order—be replaced?

(Sources, forebears, recollections, reflections—jumbled, juxtaposed; uncertainly adjudicated. Kaufman Kohler, leading light of American Reform Judaism: *Judaism does not separate religion from life, so as to regard only a segment of the common life and the national existence as holy. The entire people, the entire life, must bear the stamp of holiness and be filled with priestly consecration.* . . . Mordecai Kaplan, leader of American Jewish religious naturalism: *But when one abandons the idea of supernatural revelation, what becomes of religion? If religious truth is independent of any historic self-revelation of God to a particular people, then it is no different from scientific truth.* . . . Samson Raphael Hirsch, founder of neo-Orthodox Judaism: *Because men had eliminated God from life, nay, even from nature, and found the basis of life in possessions and its aim in enjoyment, deeming life the product of the multitude of human desires.* . . . Abraham Isaac Kook, classical Judaist: *The Light of Israel is not a utopian dream, or some abstract morality, or merely a pious wish and a noble vision. It does not wash its hands of the material world and all its values, abandoning the flesh.* . . . Edmond Fleg, historical mystic: *People ask me why I am a Jew. It is to you that I want to answer, little unborn grandson. I am a Jew because, born of Israel and having lost her, I have felt her live again in me, more living than myself. I am a Jew because, born of Israel and having regained her, I wish her to live after me, more living than in myself. I am a Jew because the promise of Israel is the universal promise. I am a Jew because* . . .)

Usually an hour or two of this was enough to drive him up a wall, for he found his interpretations (much less written notes) either philosophical hash or sophomoric stew and both depression and anger his pen. Through it all, in the living room or the tiny kitchen, Miriam read almost incessantly, and ate chocolate-covered cherries by the pound, and stared—he knew—all the proverbial holes through him. He drank a great deal.

He hadn't seen Jelly since they'd parted. He deliberately avoided both Bourbon and St. Peter streets, rarely venturing beyond Royal. He was kept informed of her, however. Shy came by the Carousel occasionally.

"How's the thirty-six-year-old dropout?"

"Tolerable, Shy. Just tolerable."

"So's she."

"Oh?"

"Gettin a awful lot of attention though. Ever since that day she run bareass on the terrace. Seems half of N'Awlins seen her."

"She's well?"

"I reckon. Havin trouble with her right foot though."

"Oh? What's wrong?"

"It's wore out from kickin the shit outa you."

"I did what I had to do."

"Sure. Moses wouldn't of done it no diff'rent. See you 'round, Jack."

Nights dragged, passed. He played, sang, drank heavily between sets. Ironically, his drawing power was more solid than ever. The applause, after every number, if not deafening, was long and warm. He acknowledged it with his now famous smile (at least in New Orleans) and sang on—with relish if not heart. Heart was hopelessly at bay in a mad apartment on St. Peter, an antiseptic motel room in Mannerville, a covert bayou grove, a . . .

" 'Impossible Dream,' Jack!"

" 'Autumn Leaves,' Jack!"

" 'Sounds of Silence,' Jack!"

" 'Love . . .' "

Pack up all my care and woe,
Here I go . . . singing low,
Bye Bye Blackbird

Where somebody waits for me,
Sugar's sweet . . .

". . . *Uch-savtom al m-zuzos baysecho uvishorecho. L-ma-an tizkru va-aseesem esa kol mitzvosoy v-hiyeesem k-dosheem laylohaychem. Anee Adonoi elohaychem.*"

("Thou shalt love the Lord, Thy God, with all thy heart, with all thy soul, and with all thy might. And these words, which I command thee this day, shall be upon thy heart. Thou shalt teach them diligently unto thy children and shalt speak of them . . .")

Choking on it.

She had left Mannerville's Temple Isaiah sanctuary (quietly, unobtrusively; every eye in the back of every head in the congregation following her long, shapely, sinful legs out) in the middle of the *kaddish* of that Friday night service in June. He himself, even in the midst of prayer, had watched her leaving with an untenable mixture of fury and desire.

"She's the talk of the temple," Miriam had said as they drove home. "And Bertha Gratz—you know that mouth of hers—has told everybody that she comes to your office. Is she—*whatever* she is—is she converting, Jacob? What is it?"

"She's interested in . . . religions," he'd replied; lamely, to be sure. "Beyond that, I don't . . ."

"She came up and said something very cryptic to me a few weeks ago, Jacob. Just before services. She said—I wish I could remember it exactly—she said—well, something to the effect—'You're very fortunate, Mrs. Weiss. Your husband's not only a rabbi, he's a man.' Isn't that odd, Jacob?"

"I suppose," he said. "I can't imagine. Kids today . . ."

Several days later the president of the congregation, Aaron Schindler, had had him to lunch at the Bayou De Jeune Country Club.

"Rabbi, I know this is ridiculous but it seems you've been . . . well, observed at a motel or two with . . . well, with that girl who . . . This is embarrassing, really. Lord knows, Rabbi, none of is . . . Hell, man. Whatever you choose to call it we got a community to think about, a *Jewish* community . . ."

It was summer in Mannerville. The kind of summer that only a Deep South town can absorb. It was created for it.

In and around Mannerville there are at least a hundred lakes and bayous, not to mention the omnipresent Shamatau River, and in summer they are jewels of time. Blue Bayou—man-imagined, man-engineered—is perhaps the zircon among them, but its luster in the June sun is just as bright, just as real. However shallow, its luminous surface puts stars in the midday sky.

It was at such a time, on such a day, in a hidden grove of willow and pine at the lower end of Blue Bayou, just up from Crazy Neck Bend some ten or twelve miles from Mannerville, that they sat together, he and Jelly, like undiscoverable children in an undiscovered room, in the tall hot grass. (Jelly's idea. Motels, even as distant as Vicksburg or Natchez or Shreveport, were out. This spot, she'd assured him, was unknown even to—"Guess Who?"). Gazing, in one of their rare, reflective times (or so he thought) upon the blinding water, sky, world.

". . . and you have to stay away from the synagogue, Jelly. You have to stop coming to Friday night services."

"Why?"

"Oh for heaven's . . ."

"I have to see you."

"You *see* me. Now. Here. You can't just . . ."

"I like you with your clothes on too."

"You're mad. Do you know that? You're really mad."

"Billygoat! I'm in love."

"And I'm not sure I can take it much longer."

"Take what?"

"You. This."

"Fuck. And don't make a face like Isaiah, or whoever's your patron saint—patron *rabbi?* Fuck's the only word for it. Kiss me."

"Jelly, you're . . ."

"Yes. Whore and harlot and . . . what are those other biblical words for me?"

"Jelly! We were talking about . . ."

"Hypocrisy. Of course. We always do. We just never give it its right name. We simply . . ."

"This may be our last time together. I mean that, Jelly. It could be our last . . ."

"Sure. Take off your pants."

"My what?"

"Your pants. Trousers. Slacks. Oh for Christ sake, Jack, we're goin swimmin in the raw, we're goin to behave like . . . I've got the word for it! Children of God. Now vomit on that one!"

"Jelly, it's still open out here . . ."

"No. Closed. Private. Ours. Eden. Now off with 'em."

"You outrageous child . . ."

"Off!"

Strange; not strange. Playing, not playing; laughing, not laughing. Touching, not touching. Touched.

"Do fish have membrane, Jack?"

"Of course."

"But not memory. Not memory."

"No. Instinct. It survives memory."

"I love water."

"Yes."

"Water. Sun."

"Yes."

"You."

"I know."

"You, you, you! Odd."

"What?"

"Your cock. Under water it feels both heavier and lighter, both at the same time. With me it's different. I'll bet you can't tell where the water ends and I begin, right?"

"Wrong."

"Oh Christ that's gorgeous! I just thought of a game."

"Game?"

"Sure. All children play games. Specially naked children in water. Would you like to know the name of it?"

"What?"

"Copulatin Catfish."

"*What?*"

"Copulatin Catfish. Groovy, hunh? At one with all the rest, all of the fun-fin creatures, all of the beautiful, unworried, un—"

"Jelly, we can't, not here, it's . . ."

"Shut up. Just shut up and copulate, you big old fish, you beautiful fish, just . . ."

Yes. Yes and yes and yes. Holding her to him, his hands

firm on her buttocks, her legs full around him, squeezing life from his unmaneuverable middle—and impossible. Happy and funny and fierce and impossible, overcome in laughter and frustration by the thick brown water, the soft giving sand; at last racing back to the place beneath the trees, a blanket on the tall grass, the feel and sound and wonder of their wetness . . .

"Wow! That's all I can say. Wow!"

"Yes. Wow."

"Jack, Jack, I think I'd die if you ever . . . Tell me somethin, good sir. How does it feel to have just deflowered the flower of Southern Christian womanhood?"

"Lovely. Very lovely."

"Thank you."

"You're welcome. Now get dressed."

"Why? I'm in no hurry."

"Jelly . . .!"

"Let's let the sun dry us off and then we can . . ."

"Shhh."

"What?"

"I thought I heard something, a motor, something . . ."

"From the road? Don't be silly, it's too far. Lordy! Ain't that just like a male catfish now. Takes his pleasure, then . . ."

"There *was* something, there, in that grove of trees, I'm certain . . ."

"A deer or somethin. They have deer out in Crazy Neck, didn't you know that? Thousands of them. Thousands and thousands . . ."

But it would haunt him. Through the long night, the days . . . Faces. Vague, indefinable, but *faces*. And one of them . . . no, surely, it couldn't have been, he was simply dulled by afterlove. Timmy? Timmy Rappaport? From his confirmation class, the Youth Group? *Timmy Rappaport . . .?*

"Jelly, please, we'd best be going."

"No."

"I said yes. Now, please . . . What in hell are you doing?"

"Decoratin it. You. Like Lady Chatterley did to the gamekeeper. Only all I have is grass and pine needles. But we all need some kind of religion, right? And this is mine. To worship at the altar of phallic . . ."

"Stop it!"

"Never. Do you have any idea how much I love you, Jack? Any idea at all? Well, I'll tell you. Enough to kill myself if it came right down to it. If I couldn't see you, touch you. Enough, you sonofabitch, to buy a gun or pills or . . ."

No one here can love and understand me.
Oh, what hard luck stories they all hand me.

Make my bed and light the light,
I'll arrive late tonight.
Blackbird, bye bye.

CHAPTER TEN

His father died at the end of April and they flew, he and Miriam (she unmistakably now with child; uneasily, defensively), to Dallas.

Sam met them at the airport. His shoulders were slumped and his face swollen from tears.

"You never knew him through these last years the way I did, Jacob. *Mensch,* such a *mensch.* Such a good decent man. Good decent man. It hurts, it truly hurts. What's that passage from *Job,* Jacob? 'But man dieth, and wasteth away: Yea, man giveth up the ghost, and where *is* he?' Is that it?"

"Yes," said Jacob, looking out the window of the Lincoln Continental at the seemingly unlimited, unmemorable Texas countryside; the unabashed immodesty of industrial Dallas.

"A good man, a good father, a good Jew. That's what everybody who knew him is saying. What greater tribute to a human being can there be, Jacob? What finer value at the end of a life, Miriam? Well, he's at peace now. And with God, with Yahweh, Who was never very far from his thoughts or his lips. From his deeds for that matter. With his beloved God . . ."

The house was as it had always been, time immemorial. a many-gabled, many-shuttered affair—a somber anachronism even when it was built, years before Jacob was born. Set back from a wide lawn in one of the older, now mostly seedy, residential streets of Dallas, it seemed not so much the symbol of a time, an age, as it did the penultimate fancy of a thousand years' ghetto dreams. His father had remained in it, among oversized sofas and chairs and outrageous tapestries of a Europe two hundred years ago—a Europe imagined, attained—even in the lame last years of his life (with an elderly Negro housekeeper whose fantasies were not dissimilar), even though Sam and Esther had cajoled him time and again to come to them in their modern, if no less modest, mansion in Hillcrest, one of the newer, more elegant sections of the city.

"He wanted to die here," said Sam, sadly. "It gave him peace to die here."

For Jacob the house, like the interminable hours he had now to spend in it, was a dull kaleidoscope of remembered names, unremembered faces; old Jews, new Jews (all Jews? Who could say; for very long even wonder?); a mumbled, murmured coming and going; English, Yiddish, German, even Russian and Italian and Greek—the infinite, finite tongues of time, the too effusive or too hollow expressions of sentiment and sympathy (and more often than not, talk of baseball or politics or business or the economy in general—those precious New World phenomena, thank God—that give purpose to the living in the face of death; affirmation of life in the fear of death; reality, for death is always unreal)—expressions as deep, and as shallow, as life-death, death-life. Amid mountains of food, oceans of liquor. Esther through it all the matriarch of time, of the Jewish experience, the Jewish vitality . . .

"Everyone all right? Another corned beef sandwich? Honest to God, the food in this place!"

Sam. Visibly saddened, assigned by divine right to humble dignity, living reverence . . .

Miriam. Speaking when spoken to; gently, quietly. Near with child, the rabbi's wife . . .

The rabbi. How many knew? The children, yes—Myron and Hannah—nephew and niece he knew hardly at all; eying him curiously, suspicioulsy, as children will; must. Ex-rabbi? Ex-convict!

(Howie Epstein of all people, forgotten, remembered: "Jeez, Jack, how many years? Good to see you, guy, good to see you. How's the rabbi trade? Seriously, fella, it's a real pleasure to see you. Even under these . . . unfortunate circumstances. You know you have my deepest sympathy, Jack. Deepest condolences. Been a long time, Jack, hasn't it? Yeah, long time. Say, Jack, remember . . . ?")

. . . a panoply of things to remember, things to forget.

Sam between people in a far corner of the dreary kitchen. "You're a pretty wealthy man now, Jacob. You know? Papa did well by you. You don't have to sing for your supper any longer, Jacob. Not that you ever had to. Oh hell, Jacob, come on. Stay here with me, the business is going great, really great, we can . . ."

Esther between drinks in a corner of an even drearier hallway. "You know something, Jacob? You really want to know something? And it's not just because I've had a couple of drinks. But you know something, Jacob? Dear brother-in-law Jack? You're a shit. God forgive me but you're a real . . . ."

A panoply.

Somewhere, at some time, at some place in the city—Gutterman's Funeral Parlor? Gutzman's?—he was alone in a long, forbidding (still, flower-decked) room with the remains of his father; the careful, costly, restored remains; stern, unforgiving, forgiving; face of a father, face of a stranger.

A dead stranger.

"Your son has come to say good-bye to you, Papa. Your son Jacob. Your son Jacob who turned his back on the ways of his father, and his father's Father. Your son Jacob, your Yonkel, pride of your loin, good Jewish boy from good Jewish stock, voice of an angel, Papa . . . remember? Good Jewish boy with a head, a heart, so stuffed with confused thoughts, impersonal dreams, that he gave himself over so early, so early, into the hands of him, Him, the Heavenly Father, only to realize so late . . . You were there, Papa, you were always there. I loved you, I know. Loved you as a presence, a force, a . . . But as a person, Papa? I cannot tell you. I cannot tell myself. I do not know. I know there are tears in my eyes . . . in my chest, my heart . . . tears that will not come again. But are they for you, Papa? Are the tears for you? You who spent your three score years and ten believing, who have passed from this earth believing . . . ? I'm not sure, Papa. I don't believe so, Papa. I believe they are for me, Papa, these tears, these long-held tears. For me, Papa, your son Jacob, Papa, pride of your loin, Papa . . . "

He cleared his eyes with a handkerchief and, true to his word, wept no more—not through the long, mournful service, not during the interminable drive to the cemetery, not at the graveside itself.

"He's heartless, *heartless!*" he heard Esther whisper to Sam, who was visibly shaken and whose tears were very real.

They slept together that night, he and Miriam, in the same bed, a great canopied affair that had been the house's guest-room pride since he could remember. It was large enough, wide enough, that they could lay without touching.

But sleep was more complicated.

"Jacob?"

"Yes?"

"He must have been a good man, your father."

"He was."

"You hate me, don't you?"

"Miriam, it's been a trying day. Try to sleep . . ."

"I had to come back, Jacob. There was no other way."

"I know."

"Now *you* will be a father."

"Yes."

"You'll resent it. Whatever it is. Boy, girl . . . you'll resent it. With no love in a home, how can there be . . . ?"

"Miriam. Sleep. This isn't the time . . ."

"We could stay here in Dallas, Jacob. You own half the business now. Eleven delicatessens. It's hard to believe, isn't it? You're a wealthy man, Jacob. The child will never want."

"No."

"Sam put it amusingly. He said, 'Miriam, your husband no longer has to sing for his sup—' "

"Go to sleep, Miriam. Please."

She touched the tips of his fingers, the most she'd dare.

"Perhaps it will be different, Jacob, when we're here awhile. When you're sitting *shiva* . . ."

"I'm not sitting *shiva.* We're flying back tomorrow."

"Tomorrow?"

"Tomorrow."

And with the great bounty of corned beef and liverwurst and pastrami to separate them, they slept.

The flight back to New Orleans was remarkably short; long and excruciating.

CHAPTER ELEVEN

Early in May, Miriam's Aunt Corinne, from Louisville—sixtyish, spinsterish—came to stay with them, "to see the baby through." She was a small, fine-boned woman, as frail in body and face as Miriam, a sympathetic if rather too saccharine soul whose favorite expression—"Oh! I think I'm going to have a heart attack!"—made no distinction between a shocking headline in the *Times Picayune* and an accidentally dropped egg on the kitchen floor. Jacob liked her actually, although her interminable chatter was not the kindest of companions to his nervous system:

"Jacob dear, you look so tired, so drawn. You don't sleep enough, you simply don't sleep enough. Does he, Miriam dear? He don't sleep enough. My dear adorable mama used to say that sleep is *not* the food of fools, contrary to whatever they say, sleep is *not* the food of . . ."

"Jacob, dear, don't you think Miriam looks sweet tonight? That maternity dress is such a . . . Oh! That dish just *flew* out of my hands. Oh! I think I'm going to have a heart attack! I'm sorry, I'm so sorry . . ."

"Jacob, dear, can you pass the turnips? My how I do crave turnips. Always have. Mama used to say they were the colored folks' magic, isn't that silly, the way myths like that just pass on from generation to generation. Now, back in Louisville . . ."

"Jacob, dear, when you and our dear Miriam move into a larger house . . ."

("What larger house? Who said anything about a larger house?")

"Why, I just took it for granted now that you've inherited all that money . . . Oh dear, I've offended you, haven't I? I have, I've offended you. And all I meant was . . . Oh! I think I'm going to have a heart attack! All I really . . ."

"Jacob dear, you simply need to put some meat on those bones. I swear, you don't eat enough to keep a bird . . ."

"Jacob dear, I said a little prayer for you in synagogue last night. A silent little prayer, all to myself. I know it don't mean anything to you anymore but . . ."

"Jacob dear, I hope I don't get on your nerves or anything, all I ever want is to be good and kind and not in anybody's way . . ."

". . . this afternoon, Jacob dear . . . Miriam dear . . . and I met this perfectly lovely lady from New Pontchartrain Street, just five blocks away, and she says the A and P is definitely the best place to shop in this . . . Oh! Did you see that black cat just pass outside the door? Oh! I think I'm going to have a heart attack! Lord knows I'm not superstitious or anything like that but I . . ."

"Jacob dear . . ."

He began staying away from the house more and more frequently, spending long afternoons rehearsing new material at the Carousel, or reading and making occasional notes at the public library, or on a bench in Jackson Square in the fine spring light; always alone, and always deep in thought, even at its most amorphous.

It was on one of the Jackson Square afternoons—he was strolling aimlessly, the sun was warm and spongy—that he saw her. She was on a crude wooden stool behind a tall rickety easel in a corner of Pirate's Alley. He only saw a fragment of her—the left side of her face; her long, restless legs in bright green slacks. She was totally absorbed in the quick light strokes of some watercolor or other. Several tourists stood looking on. She didn't look up, or if she did by chance glimpse him gave no indication of it, and he walked on quickly. The pounding in his chest was all but audible. Perhaps it *was* audible, for he was certain that every passerby stared curiously back at him, and even his shoes sounded like horses' hooves on the hot pavement.

He was perspiring heavily when he reached the Carousel. A straight shot of bourbon made him perspire even more, but it calmed him. Stoically—or if not stoically, defiantly—he started rehearsing. Only Joe Capella and the two bartenders, in one of their daily disputes over jigger generosity, were visible in the room; the place wouldn't open for another hour or so. Jacob took no notice of them, or of the place itself. He simply threw himself, in the confining emptiness that seemed as vast as a concert hall, into "Yesterday." "Dulcinea," "Take My Hand for a While," "There Is Not a Day I Did Not Love You," "Delilah," "Baby, It's Me"—songs he was adding to the repertoire.

"Man, you're poundin 'em in there today, Jack," one of the bartenders called over.

"Hot time in the old town tonight," the other one crowed.

"Finally gettin the message, eh, Reb?" Joe Capella added hoarsely. "Rockin it ain't without class neither, you know."

"*Ain't That A Shame,*" "*Applause*" . . .

Somewhere in the middle of one of them the phone rang. It was for him.

Shy.

"Hey there, Jack. Hoped I might find you there. Listen, baby, I saw you over by the Square today. I was right near Jelly. I waved. Reckon you didn't see me."

"No. No, I didn't."

"You walked by so fast."

"Yes."

"She looks great, don't she?"

"Who?"

"Who you think? Jelly!"

"Yes, Yes, she does."

"First time you seen her? I mean since . . ."

"Yes."

"Looks great, don't she?"

"I believe we've already agreed on that, Shy. Yes."

"Know why?"

"I beg your pardon?"

"I said you know why?"

"Why what, Shy?"

"Why she looks so great, what else are we talkin about?"

"I'm sure she's doing quite well."

"O.K. O.K. Play it cool, baby. Old Shy'll just have to

fill in the spaces. She looks great 'cause she's gettin it regler again."

"I'm sorry, Shy, I don't think I quite . . ."

"Regler, man, beddy steady. Jeez! You ain't dense, Jack, what the shit . . ."

"Exactly what did you call to tell me, Shy?"

"Awright, awright, so I'll plow it. You know Skip Barry? Big blond guy works the Old Absinthe House at night?"

"I don't believe, no."

"Young guy, muscles all the way to his crotch? Anyway, he's the cat moved in with her and . . ."

"I'll see you, Shy."

Jacob hung up. And back at the piano was a mountain of suppressed rage: Jack White, King of the Keyboard, Sorcerer of Song . . .

If ever I would leave you . . .

". . . and all my life, Jack, all my life. All these years. And not to find out *who* I am. Lord! That's nothin but ladies' magazine crap. You're a *who* just by being born, just by livin, growin. And not to blow my mind tryin to figure out *why* I am either. That's just as unproductive as who I am. But the . . . the *wonder* of *I am.* That's what's important, that's what's true. The pure, uncomplicated, biological, physical *wonder!* Of now, this minute, you. Of this . . . and this . . . and this . . . of me . . . of you . . . of us . . . of . . . Of a simple, beautiful, chemical wonder . . ."

"Is there any world inside you or outside you that isn't physical, Jelly? Ever?"

"Billygoat! That's one of the vomitin things about religion. Always tryin to separate emotions, turn emotions into duties, whip up duties into lists. One two three. Love of God, love of country, love of parents, love of . . . This one first, that one second, the next one . . . Horseshit! If yaw'll pardon my French. Jack, it's all here, all now, all this. A wonder that you don't have to thank anyone for, or anything for, that you don't owe anything to, that you just accept, and revel in, and . . ."

"That is hardly the most original thought in creation, young lady. I believe if you'll read . . ."

"Read, schmeed. Of course it's not an original thought. But that's beside the point. Nothin's original until *you* experience it. Then it's original. As original and innocent as the day you were born. Because this much I can tell you, darlin . . ."

"Jelly?"

"Don't interrupt me. I'm on a real trip . . ."

"Jelly, tell me something. Do you ever go out with . . . with others? I mean . . . well, with boys your own age."

"Sometimes. Sure. Though don't ask me why. To have somethin to do I suppose. Mannerville boys bore the piss out of me."

"I see."

"You do? Good. Now there's an emotion we can tackle together, Rabbi. Jealousy. Would you believe it, Rabbi? I actually looked it up in the dictionary a couple of days ago. I'm very jealous of your wife, you know. Now let's see. Jealousy is that quality of bein watchful or solicitous in guardin or keepin, of bein resentfully suspicious of a rival or a rival's influence. How's that for girl-brain? And now that my lover has at last and openly expressed it too . . ."

"Oh come on. I simply wondered."

Wondered? Simply wondered? Had it come so far? Had it really come so far?

"Simply wondered, my ass. You're crazy mad jealous, you delicious thing you, and you know it! Oh Jack, Jack, you darlin horse's ass you. Now I dare you to tell me what you told me last Wednesday. I dare you!"

"What I told you last Wednesday? What did I tell you last Wednesday?"

"That it was the last time, that we just couldn't go on this way, that . . . Last Wednesday, and the Wednesday before, and . . ."

"This Wednesday. Yes. Perhaps it's good you did bring it up, Jelly. Because it's true, you know. There are some things in this life that . . ."

"That what? That what? All right, baby, if it makes you feel any better then go on and make like it *is* the last time. The very last last last last time. Enter me with a thousand sweet good-byes, a thousand thousand groovy good-byes, a thousand thousand . . . Oh lord, lord, right now I believe, I believe, I *do* believe! You *are* the chosen people, you *are,* you *are. . . .*"

This time it had taken place in the back seat of her car in a grove of fruitwood trees at Badger's Lake, another of Mannerville's distant Edens. And from its excitement, its depletion, its haunting lunacy, he had emerged more shaken, more shamed (more senselessly in love!) than ever.

It was a summer of infinite unrest; of infinite disorientation. Of resoluteness, irresoluteness. A summer of personal uncertainty, professional disenchantment. A summer of both intellectual and emotional dishonesty, disharmony. A summer of . . .

Had it really begun in earnest then—that summer in

Mannerville? The self-appraisal, self-contempt? The now all-too-real dissatisfaction, discomfort with ritual; the emptiness, fullness (hypocrisy? fear?) that saw him stranger to the Sabbath? Stranger to synagogue, to congregation, to Mannerville, to Miriam—to himself? To his journal—where no entries were made, could possibly be made? Where . . .

That summer. That summer when—outside Jelly—nothing but his sermons (dull, innocuous) and the Youth Group meetings (pale and uninvolving except for Timmy Rappaport, whose eyes, while never directly upon him, were never very far from him) occupied most of his time and thought. That summer when two deaths in the congregation called upon energies and emotions he seemed incapable of. That summer when he and Miriam journeyed to New York for a rabbinical conclave and symposium where he saw old classmates, old friends, old teachers, old mentors—and responded to each in turn, to all in conference, with practiced tongue, imprisoned heart. That summer when the typewritten poem (surely Timmy Rappaport's) was folded carefully between the pages of the oversized Friday night service prayer book on the desk in his study: *These things too shall come to pass, Eleventh Commandment for the rabbi's ass.* That summer when . . .

"I don't know how it happened, Jelly, when it happened, why it happened, but it has to *un*happen, we have to . . ."

"What, Jack? We have to what? *Un*love? Billygoat! We have to *un*wind, that's what we have to do. We have to weigh Ethics with Eros, we have to . . . Don't think I ain't—*haven't*—been readin up a storm too, darlin. We have to . . . We have to be us, Jack. *Us.* We have to grab small beauty in all the large ugliness, we have to . . . You're right, Jack. Fuck me. Fuck me good and proper . . ."

Hot summer. Summer of . . .

"Jacob. I know about it, Jacob. About the girl, the *shikse*. God, dear God, if we had a child, if we could have a child. A child would . . ."

"Miriam. Miriam, listen, please. I'm not certain I can function any longer as a rabbi. I'm not certain I even . . ."

Making an entry in his journal after so many sterile weeks.

August 28.

I know, I must know, that Jelly came to me at a time of strain, stress. That Jelly is not the reason, simply the rhyme. The catalyst. The cunt-catalyst, as she would say, as she would laugh. As she . . .

I don't know when, where, God only knows why, this alteration, this metamorphosis, took place in me. Was my head, as a boy, so in the clouds? Did the daily ordinariness of a rabbi's life eat away at me, take its toll? (I do know this: One more marriage, one more funeral, one more confirmation, one more briss, one more trivial squabble of the Board, one more congregant talking about the "uppity niggers," and I'll climb walls!)

Was it always just a Theatricality in me, never Thought? Or, if Thought—the esoteric, the impersonal? Was it always . . . ? I don't know myself. I never knew myself.

Miriam. Was it Miriam? Is it Miriam? The day-after-day, night-after-night kosher sound of her, sense of her?

Jelly. Jelly. Opening windows, tearing down walls. Oh God, I need her. I do . . .

And can't. Won't. Know I can't, won't. Know I . . .

" . . . larger congregation, Miriam, maybe that's what I need. A larger congregation, a city. Maybe that's . . ."

"Yes, Jacob. Go to sleep, Jacob. Sleep. Summer will soon be over."

Summer.

"Billygoat! You know what it says in that prayer book of yours, baby? In one of those silent prayers 'as the heart may prompt'? It says, 'As a child yields itself to lovin arms, I yield myself to Thee, askin for nothin, complainin about nothin. What if my labor is hard, what if my lot is humble, what if my dreams turn into futile tears, if only there is the peace of Thy nearness in my heart.' That's what it says. Billygoat, billygoat, horseshit! There's the nearness of *us, us,* now, *us* . . ."

Summer. A season. Five thousand seasons. As the crow flies. As the Jew walks.

Runs.

Quietly, desperately, through the Hebrew Union College in Cincinnati, he'd managed to secure a pulpit in New Orleans.

"It will be better there, Jacob, you'll see, you'll see. Once we're away from this . . . this evil . . ."

And the glorious beauty which is on the head of the fat valley shall be a fading flower, and as the hasty fruit before summer.

He hadn't told her he was leaving. He hadn't seen her again until a summer later when she'd breezed into his study at B'nai Israel on St. Charles in New Orleans, as though the Mannerville summer itself had never passed.

"Hi there, coward. I figured the dog days needed a few blind puppy hours . . ."

Summer.

Summer of . . .

Love is a many-splendored . . .

"Swing it, Jack!"

"Talk to me, baby!"

"Give it soul, Jack!"

"Tell it like it is, hon!"

That night (the next? two nights later? three?), he ran into her a half block down from the Carousel; in the small dark hours of the morning. She was all laughter and light in a thigh-length leather skirt, knee-high leather boots, her blonde hair long and free and affirmative. The man with her (Man? Boy!) was just as blond, just as loose, just as undaunted. They were both high on something—liquor, pot, themselves—something.

"Jack White—I mean *Jacob Weiss*—meet Skip Barry. Big bastard, ain't he? Better be, darlin. He's ballin me now."

Laughing over her shoulder, a block away, a mile, no more than a heartbeat, "Oh . . . in case I forgot to say it . . . Good-bye, Rabbi."

Jelly . . .

Part Four

✡ ✡ ✡ ✡ ✡ ✡ ✡ ✡

CHAPTER TWELVE

"I don't know. Whole world's crazy these days. If it ain't riots and wars it's dope and porno. And if it ain't them it's niggers actin like they was white folks havin to grub like they was niggers. Just don't make sense. Don't make no sense no whichaways. Like I said to Mumsie—that's the old lady, real name's Lureen Sue—Mumsie, I said, it just don't make sense. Not that I ain't proud to to have you birthin another one for me but Mother Mary a seventh mouth to feed! A seventh sweet innocent babe to bring into this sonofabitchin—I didn't say that to Mumsie now, don't get me wrong. Mumsie's a lady, a real fine lady, and she's got real sensibilities, you know? But shit fire it's one hell of a thing, a seventh goldern . . . Your first ain't it?"

"I'm sorry," said Jacob, "I . . . I suppose I was off somewhere. You were saying . . . ?"

"Your first. I was inquirin if you was waitin on your first."

"Yes. Yes, my first."

"Knowed it. Knowed it right off. You can aw-ways tell. Man gets them glazed eyes, mind off somewheres in sugar cane country . . . You can tell. Well, I don't mean to be no pestamist or nothin, because I believe with all my heart in the Good Christ Aw-mighty, but here's hopin there's a world worth being birthed in for both our sweet innocent . . ."

They were at a back table in the crowded cafeteria of Touro Hospital, he and—O'Connell? O'Connor? Why had he even accepted the man's invitation for a cup of coffee, a slice of pie? And he knew if he didn't get away, and shortly, he would go stir.

"There will be a world," he said. "Whatever it is. Whatever we make it. All good things to you." And fled back to the obstetrics floor.

Where Aunt Corinne, patiently knitting in a sitting room, offered little more than a variation on a theme.

"Jacob dear, you must compose yourself. It's goin to be a long hard labor, the doctor's already prepared me. Miriam's such a frail thing, more's the pity. Just like her dear mama and my dear mama and . . . Well, all of us on the Lowenstein side, we're just naturally . . . It's goin to be a real long siege of it, dear, now why don't you go off somewheres, walk around for a little while, you look so tired and drawn. There's nothin to worry about, Jacob dear, nothin at all to . . ."

Downstairs again, and out.

It was a humid afternoon. One of those gray June days in New Orleans when the heat itself seems to take on the day's color. Rain threatened, but denied. The people walking the streets, as well as those in passing vehicles, looked as if they were propelled by some gaseous energy not their own.

Jacob walked. He wasn't certain where. It didn't matter where. He was conscious of the heat, of the grayness. Even in his summerweight suit he was a pond of perspiration. It didn't matter. The very awareness of motion, of purely physical movement, was more involving.

Hours later (fifteen minutes? twenty?) he found himself in front of a synagogue, a Conservative one, Zichron Ephraim, one he knew of, one whose rabbi—Harry Pollock—he had spoken with at various functions, one whose location he was not unfamiliar with. Was it by chance he stood there, paused there? That he entered? It didn't matter. It was a long, thought-bending, nerve-stretching, hot, gray day.

It was as warm inside, if not warmer. The sanctuary—a small, very old room of worship, with stained-glass windows depicting the Exodus and a plain, traditional ark and hard fruitwood pews with thin, faded cushions—was stifling. And quite dark. Jacob sat (self-consciously, he had to admit; even alone) in a rear corner.

It was strange: being there, sitting there: not certain of what he felt, didn't feel. A spirituality? Yes, that. Aloneness in sepulchral quiet imposes upon even the most hardened unbelievers that. But a spirituality of heaven . . . ?

(". . . and when we have nowhere else to turn, darlin, then we'll just roll over and say our prayers to What's-his-face. Yeah. God. But not God-God, not Him-God. No. We'll roll over, like this . . . like this, my beautiful goddamn love, my always so serious, never less than sensational, inscrutable goddamn love, and we'll say our prayers to Room-God and Bed-God and Jelly-God and Jack-God . . .")

How long ago? How . . . ?

"I want the child. With all my heart I want the child. I want the life of the child. I want the loveliness of the child. I want Miriam's health and her safety. I want the joy of her motherhood. Whatever I am or have become, whatever I do or fail to do, whatever I cry for in dreams, I want . . .

"Jelly, I want . . ."

Rain? Rain on the roof?

"Jack? Jack Weiss? I thought it was you, I wasn't sure. It's so dark in here. I was in my study and I heard a voice . . ."

"How are you, Harry?"

Rabbi Harry Pollock, a thin, rather dyspeptic-looking man in his late forties, early fifties (face like parchment long since soaked, long since dried), answered with the intruder's unease, "Fine, Jack. I was . . . well, as I said, I was . . ."

"I hadn't realized I was speaking aloud," said Jacob; starting to rise.

Harry Pollock shifted—the weight of his voice as well his feet. It was lower, even more indecisive.

"Please . . . please. I'm delighted to see you. Surprised, naturally, but . . . delighted. Well."

"Yes," said Jacob. "Well."

The rabbi sat beside him. "I must say," he said, "I would never have expected . . . that is, I had thought . . . I mean heard . . ."

"The rumors of my death have been greatly exaggerated, Harry," Jacob smiled, half-smiled, in the shadows. "Besides. It's raining out, isn't it?"

"Is it?" Harry Pollock shifted again—this time, buttocks—uncomfortably. "I hadn't noticed."

"This is a very pleasant synagogue, Harry," said Jacob. "And built well, I must say. The acoustics are first-rate."

"I apologize for disturbing you, Jack. I know you wouldn't be here if you hadn't wanted to be . . ."

"Alone? Relax, Harry. None of us is a stranger to that."

Harry Pollock cleared his throat. "Is there any way I can help you, Jack? You know I would be only too . . ."

"I didn't come here for help," said Jacob. "But thank you anyway . . . Rabbi."

Even in the darkness Jacob could see the thin, bloodless face moving from side to side. "You're a confused man, aren't you, Jacob Weiss? Jack White?"

Jacob stood up. "I would sincerely hope so," he said.

Harry Pollock stood too. "This isn't the Crescent Carousel, Jack. I'm not sitting at a piano bar where genuine sentiments are treated with flip . . ."

"I'm sorry, Harry," said Jacob, starting to move past him. "I *was* being flip, forgive me. *Sholom Elechom.* Good things for you, Harry."

Bony, but strong—the grip on his arm. "Jack. Jacob. Yonkeleh. As do all of us, I have felt much but learned little in this life. But this much I *have* learned. The search for God is essentially the search for self. And no matter how learned we become, no matter the level of our sophistication, we're still all of us simply sophomores posing as seniors. Nothing more, Jack. Jacob."

It pursued him—down and across many city blocks, in

the still-thick gumbo air (rain yet an illusion)—an irradicable companion.

When he arrived back at the hospital, unfamiliar faces were very fiercely grim, familiar ones were very sadly sympathetic, and Aunt Corinne's simply stared into space. The baby, a boy, was stillborn.

CHAPTER THIRTEEN

Way down yonder in . . .

It had been a long night, the longest ever. Even though he was leaving the Carousel early, playing only two sets. Two sets too many, the way he sweated through them. In a corner booth, her eyes never off him, Miriam sat with her Aunt Corinne. That she was there at all was something of a miracle. Even as late as five in the afternoon her decision had been in doubt.

It had been weeks since she'd left the hospital—and just as many that she hadn't left the house. In a kind of perpetual dusk she had sat and lain, cooked and cleaned, read and watched television, moving through hours, days —interminable nights—in near-maddening gentleness, near-martyred silence, a kind of pitiful smile like a mask across her face, oddly hardening rather then softening her features. She spent an inordinate amount of time in the bathroom; crying, he knew; although her eyes never showed it. She used more makeup than she ever had before. She became obsessive about dust—on tables, lamps, chairs. She was forever jumping up to remove a spot, a speck, real or imaginary. But strangest of all, and almost without his realizing it, she no longer kept a kosher kitchen.

When she spoke to him (and of course she did; it was simply an overall behavioral pattern that sentenced her to silence) it was usually to say something like "You're very kind, Jacob" . . . "Thank you for being so understanding, Jacob" . . . "You're very good to me, Jacob" . . . "You're sweet to spend so much time at home like this, Jacob." Only once—and that obliquely—had she mentioned the child. In the dreaded darkness of their small room. "Jacob? Jacob? He's a vengeful God, too. You turned from Him, He turned from you. He made me barren . . ."

Aunt Corinne had stayed on, "to see the dear child through this ordeal." But the time had come when Aunt Corinne had to return to Louisville. It had been impulse perhaps—intuition even more?—that had prompted him even to suggest the evening out: meeting him at the Crescent Carousel (hearing him sing, for the first time *sing*), dinner at Brennan's before driving to the airport . . .

He was as cautious as a canary in his repertoire—"September Song," "Am I Blue?," "Soon It's Gonna Rain," "Try To Remember," "Follow the Fellow Who Follows a Dream"—even under the evil eye of Joe Capella, glowering from the depths of the main bar.

"Sing it, Jack!"

"Swing it, Jack!"

At Brennan's, queen of the restaurants on Royal, they dined. Indefatiguably.

Helplessly.

Miriam and her aunt had Lamb Chops *Mirabeau* (with bacon and a combination of Bernaise and tomato sauce) and he had *Caille Sur Son Nid De Printemps* (an oven-roasted quail in a potato nest, served in a Burgundy wine sauce with diced artichoke buttons over a blend of wild and white rice) and he ordered a bottle of Chateau Ste. Roseline (which mainly he consumed) and they all had Bananas Foster (with rum sauce set aflame at the table) and at every serving and with every other bite Aunt Corinne said "Oh! It's gorgeous! I think I'm going to have a heart attack!" but it was an evening somewhat less than festive. He, as well as Miriam, was almost studiedly monosyllabic, and after polite compliments on his performance, the conversation—such as it was—was left to Aunt Corinne.

"It's not easy, ever. None of it. None of it's ever easy."

"What?"

"Life."

"Oh."

"None of it. The Christians are right when they call it a vale of tears. I remember how my own dear mama . . ."

But it didn't matter. The strain of the weeks, the night, the talk and laughter at other tables, the dizzying display of flaming foods, the wine—all met to dim the moment like a theater scene behind gauze curtains; and the part of his mind that lived, saw, heard, remembered, was in another part of the world, of the volatile city, on that day she showed up at his B'nai Israel study for seemingly the hundredth time . . .

"Jelly, why do you persist? You know I left Mannerville because . . ."

"Billygoat! You know *I* left Mannerville because I'm very honestly, sincerely, very frigginly in love with you and nothin else in this mother world means a goddamn thing. And you know you're goin to take up with me again . . . it's written in the stars, darlin, if not in the Torah . . . and so why don't you just cut the shit and get on with it? I've got this absolutely sensational pad in the Quarter and I mean whoever in New Orlins would ever suspect that Rabbi Jacob Weiss of Temple whatever the hell you call it, would be . . ."

"You never let up, do you?"

"No, I don't. Not when body and soul are at stake. Jack darlin, listen. I'm a home wrecker, I'm the whore of Babyon. And I'm one determined little bitch, let me tell you. Now, kindly remove that imaginary yarmalliker you're wearing—is that what they call the thing?—and we'll . . ."

"Stop it! You're driving me up a wall and you know it. You get me so I can't even . . . Jelly, now *you* listen. I have a place in the order of things, a moral responsibility, a tradition . . ."

"Oh shut up. You have a beautiful hard-on for a broad you can't get out of your system, so get crackin. We'll go to my devilish little apartment and have a lovely little intercourse and then maybe afterwards we can talk about Martin Boober."

". . and dear Mama had a real true life philosophy about things, when you get right down to it I mean. She used to say that there's a time to live, a time to die, a time to love, a time to . . . Oh! This coffee! It's marvelous! I think I'm going to have . . ."

At the airport she waved good-bye with fond assurances that the future held lovely things, lovely things; and they were alone together, he and Miriam—on the long drive home; in the long night, day; days; nights.

Part Five

✲ ✲ ✲ ✲ ✲ ✲ ✲ ✲

CHAPTER FOURTEEN

Somehow it passed: time. June was September, September January, and the silence between them found an immunity to seasons. Jacob played on at the Carousel, wrote or made notes with painful unaccomplishment, read with near-rueful indulgence, and pursued memory or fantasy frequently. At some point in the weary months he became interested in the New Orleans Foundation for Human Betterment, a nonprofit organization with large dreams and vague plans for better housing for the poor, particularly blacks, and largely and vaguely he gave much of his time to it. Writing pamphlets mainly; soliciting funds from national corporations with branches in the city—generally by letter—occasionally. (Lose yourself in largeness to sublimate your smallness.) It was both meaningful and empty.

Miriam, too—in her own way, world—went on. She read a great deal, began to knit, crochet. She left the house as infrequently as possible, even relinquishing—with no word said—her flights to Friday night services. She said one night, soul in darkness, "Jacob, try. Try, please," and he tried. But touching her, somehow, offended them both, and he without erection, she without juices, they separated.

And in abortiveness, debasement, were silent.

The night—nights—were long.

Still, somehow it passed: time.

Sam and Esther came in late October, stayed for a week at the Royal Orleans. He and Miriam had dinner with them at Galatoire's and Arnaud's, lunch at Commander's Palace, and twice Miriam prepared meals at the house. There was talk, the semblance of talk. He could recall little of it. Except for a moment or two alone with Sam perhaps; a dialogue of sorts.

"I've tried to understand you, Jacob. Honest to God, I've tried to understand you. Maybe it's me, maybe I don't . . ."

"What's there to understand, Sam? Each of us has a choice, a will, a way. This is mine, that's all."

"All, shmall. Don't oversimplify for me, Jacob. I wasn't born yesterday neither, you know. Do you think I don't have eyes? Ears? Do you think I don't see how aimless you've become? Like driftwood you've become? And Miriam. Such a stranger, that girl. Staring off into space like . . . like she was . . ."

"The baby affected her profoundly, Sam. More than you realize perhaps. She's hardly had an easy time of it."

"That's not what I'm talking about. Do you think I don't understand about the baby? Or that Esther don't understand? Our hearts are broken too, you know. But it's more than the baby and you know it. Esther was saying it to me just last night, back at the hotel. You're not man and wife, are you, Jacob?"

"If you mean do we sleep together, do we have sexual intercourse together, no, we are not man and wife, Sam."

"Esther's right about another thing too I'll bet. You're going to pop off and leave her again, aren't you?"

"Sam, I see no reason for this, we have our own . . ."

"Such a *meshugenah* you are, such a crazy. It wouldn't any of it have been like this if you'd come back to Dallas. If you'd come home. If you'd just come home."

Home.

Somehow it passed: time.

In November, a night in November, a nightclub owner from San Francisco named Marty Fine said, "You got a style, fella. You got a yesterday-now style that moves me, moves me," and offered him the piano in his Club Cozy —"just down the hill from Nob"—which he gave thought to, serious thought to, and on which thought, excuse, he got drunk, very drunk, and at four in the morning, for the first time since he had left it, found himself on St. Peter, across the street from her apartment where a light was on (if dim) and his imagination (even dimmer) sought the two of them together—she and her beautiful blond bartender—and found them.

If not his voice.

Unless the tightness of chest is voice.

"So long as you are here, Jelly, in this city, Jelly, in this time, in this space, in this street, Jelly . . . never again the way I left Mannerville, never again the way . . ."

But then he was confused, and drunk; very drunk.

Still, it passed: time.

CHAPTER FIFTEEN

Miriam committed suicide on the fifth of February.

It was one of those tepid, unseasonal days in New Orleans, misty and vague, anticipation of Mardi Gras dense in the air He had spent most of the day in, reading, fumbling at writing (he spent more afternoons at home now, with Aunt Corinne gone); taking an hour or so to drive to one of the Metarie shopping centers for groceries, laundry. There had been nothing unusual about Miriam's day either, although in retrospect he would probably seek it. She was quiet, unobtrusive—smile a little more remote perhaps. She'd prepared an unusually large and lovely meal: roast goose with dressing, broccoli with hollandaise, a pineapple upside-down cake. But even this seemed simply a woman's need to do, be, whatever her emotional state. After complimenting her profusely (too profusely perhaps?) he had left for the Carousel.

And thoughtlessly, imprisoned by thought, played and

sung well enough to earn exceptional applause, praise. He'd had to sing "Impossible Dream" twice.

At two thirty, three, he had gone for a sandwich, coffee, a brandy, at the Dixie Dome a block or so away. When he'd arrived home at four, somewhere in the vicinity of it, he had had another brandy in the small dark dining room, then gone on to the guest room, which had been Aunt Corinne's and which in some unspoken agreement between them he now occupied. Undressed, brushed his teeth, put on his pajamas, gotten into bed. And lain awake, as was not unusual either, in his stalemated irony, affronted with the long long thoughts of youth.

But sleep, for some reason, *had* been more elusive than usual. The house's stillness, always its blessing as well as its curse, had—in night's more vulnerable nervous system—seemed strangely deathlike. And strangely, after an hour or two of sleeplessness, he had known.

Something. He had known something.

Death, even in silence, is louder than life. When he had opened the door to her room, switched on the light, it had screamed.

"*God! My God . . .*"

Paleness in death, blueness in death, pastyness in death, puffiness in death—these had gathered like warring torments in an empty bottle of pills on the night table.

She was buried in Atlanta, alongside her mother and father, and they were all there: Sam and Esther, Aunt Corinne, cousins he had barely heard of or knew only slightly, childhood friends from Atlanta. All in mournful consolation darting toward him their furtive, accusing glances. All in mournful consolation having something to say.

"A saint," said Aunt Corinne. "If dear Jewish girls can be said to be saints."

"Such a serious girl, always studying something," said one of the friends.

"Talked about having children, always talked about having children," said another of the friends.

"Never asked much of life. Never asked much of life at all," said one of the cousins.

"Such *matzoh brei* she made, I'll never forget it," said another of the cousins.

"Someone will pay, oh will someone pay," said Esther.

"God in His infinite wisdom," said Sam.

Vohavto ays Adonoi elohecho b-chol l-vovcho uvchol nafshcho uchol m-odecho. V-hoyu havdoreem . . .

It was only when he was back in New Orleans, in the house in Metarie, that the tears came: not for Miriam, not even for himself, but for waste. Simple, infinite waste. And only when he was going through bureau drawers in preparation for leaving the house (to a small apartment in the Quarter; what else? where else?), that he found among his own belongings, not hers (which the New Orleans police had necessarily, but perfunctorily, searched), her note to him; pressed carefully, if not demoniacally, against the cardboard backing of a freshly laundered shirt.

> Jacob. Dearest Jacob. I know you will dispose of this when you have read it. It is the only way, Jacob. God asked that it be this way. God of Abraham, Isaac and Jacob. Of Sarah, Ruth and Naomi. He told me it must be this way, Jacob. He came to me in the night, in the day, and He told me it must be this way. That I must die so that you might live. To sit *shiva,* Jacob. For all of us,

Jacob. To sit *shiva* for all of us, Jacob. He has not forsaken you, Jacob. He told me. He has not forsaken you. He has only forsaken me. He told me, He told me this. Oh God, Jacob, dearest Jacob, how bad you are at arithmetic. It was not your child, Jacob. I don't know whose child it was, Jacob. I only know that when you sent me to Louisville I got off in Mobile, it was as if He took my hand and led me there, and I went to a hotel and then a saloon, a bar, whatever they call it, and because I was angry or hurt or whatever poor mortals choose to call it, I got drunk, Jacob, very drunk, I who never drink, and there was a man, a Jewish man, he spoke Yiddish and laughed, laughed and laughed, and I let him come back to the hotel with me, Jacob, I

Jacob. Oh God, Jacob, don't feel guilty. Even about the girl, the *shikse,* and even if what you did was sinful, sinful. And I, Jacob, I, how I wanted a baby, a child, to have you back, Jacob, to have you need me, dearest dearest Jacob, to tell you in death what I never could in life, to

Jacob, Jacob, feel no guilt, please. And forgive me, as He, the God of Zion

In death she became the person he had not known in life. He was sick most of the night.

Day was another matter. Time became intolerable. He moved into two small furnished rooms on Dauphine Street, storing his own things, and after a week called Joe Capella to ask for an extended leave from the Carousel, where his substitute—a Negro blues singer named Flora Faye—was attracting customers in less than droves. Capella grudgingly complied, but his coarse threats of permanent replacement if he stayed away much longer were hardly heard. Nothing very much was heard. Not even the lusty sounds of the Quarter, where carnival fever was rising to a peak.

A loner for so long, he became now practically monastic, leaving the apartment only to buy food, consuming a minimum even of that. He drank as frequently as an abused stomach permitted him. He didn't shave, and his beard grew long and without shape, and the irregularity of toilet habits, of sleep, kept him in a state of almost uninterrupted lethargy. He read little, if at all; wrote not at all. Even his thoughts, such as they were (and if amorphous comings and goings of words and people, of circles and squares, can be said to be thoughts), were unremembered. But he fared; he crested the hours, days.

And then one day, a Saturday, still dulled and drowsy from sleepnessness, drink—and neither asking himself why nor wondering to ask himself why—he left the apartment and drove to a *shul,* a rigidly Orthodox *shul,* far out on Tulane. And there, among the singsong prayers of mostly old men in old, ritualistic garb, he stood and sat and as best he could, sought; something; either in intellect or emotion. But nothing touched him or offended him, pained him or pleasured him, or sought him out in return.

Except memory perhaps; strange memory for *shul.*

"Jesus, that was super, really first-rate super. Wasn't it, darlin? Wasn't it first-rate super? I think you even sexed out my esophagus. Wow! I bet your puny old wife never gave you a goin over like that. I bet . . ."

"Jelly, how many times must I tell you that my wife has nothing to do with . . ."

"Billygoat! Will you relax for cryin out loud? Lord!

You just had a fantastic sexual encounter, nut, will you just lay back and let it spoil you? Like too much cotton candy at the carnival? Too many peanuts at the circus? That's what's important, Jack. That's what we have to hold on to. The sweet feelin of Afterward when we can just sit back and glory in Before. That's what makes it all so super, don't you see? Now. Relax. Breathe soft. There. Don't you feel better? Smile."

"I'm smiling."

"You're adorable when you do, you really are. Aren't you glad I came to New Orlins? Aren't you glad I haul-assed after you?"

"You win. I'm glad."

"I love you when you're like this. I love the livin shit out of you, I really do. I love . . . Jack?"

"Mmn?"

"How did you become a rabbi?"

"Just lucky I guess."

"No, seriously, smartass."

"How did I become a rabbi. I suppose I was a rabbi even as a child, Jelly."

"Beard and all?"

"Foolish girl."

"I'm serious. I'll bet my bottom . . . well, just my bottom . . . that you don't like bein a rabbi. I'll bet you anything you don't like ministerin to other people's needs. I'll bet you anything you're too all-fired excited to be ministerin for once in your life to your own needs. I mean your *real* needs. I'll bet you . . ."

"Why don't we change the subject?"

"Why should we?"

"Because I don't really feel it's relevant to . . ."

"What? To this? Mnn!"

"To . . . well, to . . ."

"Billygoat! You're really a fraud, Jack. Do you know that? You're a great fuck but you're a fraud. And I oughta know. I've got a cunt's intuition, darlin. An *atheistic* cunt's intuition. But because you're such a sweetheart there'll be no more questions, no more . . ."

At what point in time, what place . . . in what darkness, what light?

"Darlin, face it. You know you want out. And by Out I don't mean out of *these* . . . these arms that could squeeze the bejesus out of you till the cows come home. And don't scowl like that. It's like bad light on a good paintin. You know exactly what I mean by Out. Out of somethin that's just as hokey as Daddy's Jesus-baby. Out of somethin you just mouth because it's always been and because . . .

"Did you ever have a real spiritual experience, Jack? I mean, a real soul-perspirin, mind-bendin spiritual orgasm? Because if you did, darlin, it wasn't in your *shul* or synagogue or whatever you call it. It was in bed, baby —with me—and on a riverbank—with me—and in . . .

"Jack . . . Jack darlin, it's true. This is where you belong. This little old rabbit hutch is what you really want. Leave the rest of it, darlin. The whole phony-rony. It's here you're alive, here you're . . .

"There's this place I know needs a singer, you'd be sensational, darlin, delicious. Doll you up in a tux or somethin and you'd be . . .

"Jack. Jack, don't split now. Whatever you do, don't split now. Not now. Not like you did in Mannerville. Not this time. A tushy for a Torah, it's a good bargain. Seize it, darlin, seize it. Hold onto it. All of it. This time, this place . . ."

This darkness, this light.
The thigh of a chicken negates . . .

"*Sholom Alechem.* You are troubled in yourself, my son?"

An old Jew's eyes, old Jew's breath. He fled.

Back in the apartment (in clarity, now, a pitiful victim of all the drink-lost days; as dirty, dusty, cluttered and unlivable as ever Jelly's had been) he fell into an exhausted sleep; a sleep fitfully invaded by stomach pains and hallucinations, but one nonetheless long and deep and true. When he waked, sometime in the dark early morning, it was with the certainty that his weeks as a recluse, for the moment at least, were past. And that he had to see her, touch her, hear her voice; saying something, anything: foolish, fanciful, depleting, outrageous; something.

When it was daylight, and the sounds of morning were full, he telephoned Shy. Then he showered, and very painfully, but resolutely, shaved off his beard.

CHAPTER SIXTEEN

She met him at the Den of Doves on Bienville.

Although it was a Sunday, and just past noon, it was also the time of carnival, and the small tight room (a hole in the wall actually; newly scooped-out cove, haven, for the turned-on young) was bustling and noisy. Revelers, revilers, revolutionaries—call them what you would; it couldn't have mattered less. They were an imposing presence.

Hers the most imposing of all. She sat at a small center table, rough and wobbly with its knife-carved names and initials and urinal wit, its much-abused legs; her long blonde hair combed severely back, tied in a bright orange ribbon, as she had never worn it before; tall—much taller than he remembered, or allowed himself to remember—and proud, very proud: pride (slightly impatient, almost affected; even imperious) that he had not seen before either on her lively, eager face. His heart didn't race; it literally stopped. The rest of the raucous room was instantly turned off.

Feeling oddly like a very young boy on his very first date, uncertain of what he should say, what he *would* say, he said, "Why are we meeting here?"

To which she responded, but with not the slightest trace of his own nervousness, "Just why are we meetin at all, darlin?" And a little defiantly, he thought. Felt. "Shy wasn't exactly enlightenin on that point. Why did you want to see me, Jack?"

He took the chair across from her, still awkwardly the boy, and said very softly, "To talk about getting married."

She neither stirred nor changed expression; seemed, in fact, not even to have heard it. "I'm sorry about your wife," she said. "I think I am anyway. I hear you've had yourself a real sunny holiday."

"It hasn't been easy, no."

"You've lost weight."

"Yes."

"And you're pale as a coal miner. You need some air."

"I know. And you? How are you, Jelly?"

She smiled, shrugged. "Well as can be I reckon. Up to here with waitin tables but what the hell. I'm gettin my three squares every day. And I've been sellin some of my watercolors, did you hear?"

"I'm glad," he said.

In the rather uncomfortable silence they ordered drinks from a very young girl, while the loud conversations of those around them pelted their senses. And through it all, like the score of a bad, blatant play, Moby Grape screamed from the juke box, *Ooh, Mama, ooh, Mama, ooh.*

Jacob, his voice almost a whisper in the din, said, "Jelly, I was very serious. I want you to marry me."

"And spoil a good separation?" she said.

Now he raised his voice, and knew it. "Jelly, this is hardly the time to be flip. I said . . ."

"I know what you said." And now her voice—not to mention her face, body—was full, alive. "I know somethin else too. You leave me high and dry for a woman you've already left and who you never loved in the first place, I don't care if she *is* your wife or what she's carryin in her belly, then she loses it and does herself in, you look like you haven't eaten for a month, I'm shacked up with a bartender, and you want to play third finger left hand. I'm flattered, darlin, and thanks but no thanks. The sentiment's sweet but I don't think I'm quite in the frame of mind to play Mrs. Ex-Rabbi."

He was paler, if that was possible. "This isn't like you," he said.

"Oh?"—eyes flashing as he had never seen them—"And just what *is* like me, darlin?"

He looked down, with a kind of dumbness, at his untouched drink. "Not like this," he said. "Not like this."

"Billygoat! If some of my choicer language will make it more convincin, then . . ."

"Jelly. Jelly, don't. Please." His eyes met hers with a terrible pride, a terrible shame. "If it's marriage per se that you resent," he said (stiffly? defensively?), "then we could . . ."

Her smile, even sober, seemed drunkenly crooked. "And who would you run back to next time? God?"

If his chest was hard, his voice was not. If anything, it was bleeding: "How many times have you thrown yourself at me, Jelly? Well, now I'm throwing myself at you. I love you, Jelly. I love you very much."

The break in her voice, while slight, was unmistakable.

"That's the first time you ever said that," she said. "Voluntarily, that is. Did you know that?"

"Jelly, all I know is . . ."

"Go fuck yourself. And with that, darlin, if you'll pahdon the uptown expression, I think I'll tyke a leak."

—with brave Johnny Cash in the jukebox.

She came back like a tall, proud heron; gold hot pants the blister of noon.

"If you're this bitter," he said, "why did you even agree to meet me?"

"Old times' sake, darlin," she said, "old times' sake."

He looked down again; drink untouched still. "Jelly, we're both free now to . . ."

"Billygoat! Just who do you think you are? Just because . . ."

"Does he really mean that much to you, Jelly? This . . . ?"

"His name's Skip. I call him Slip." Her laugh—half angry, half derisive—was chilling. "Oh, he's amusin, you might say. Fun to yak with, blow a little grass with. Handsome cat, hung like a mule. He's a great hump actually . . ."

When he slapped her, hard, it was noticed, but barely acknowledged, in the dizzying room. But her face, for a moment, seemed to crack like a piece of fine china, and his hand, back in his lap, trembled still with rage, outrage. In truth, the violence inside him—stranger as it was to every cell and pore—drowned out not only the room but the world.

After an eternity she said (casually? pityingly?), "It's all right, Jack. You needed it."

Standing, she towered.

"Jelly, why are you doing this? Why are you—?"

"Growin up I reckon. Try and get laid today, will you darlin? It'll put roses in your cheeks."

And incredibly he was alone, with a watery drink, a wounded mind. And somewhat bewildered eyes that passed through forests of hair, jungles of beard, and for all the long, weary journey saw nothing.

CHAPTER SEVENTEEN

But somehow—back at the old stand.

Way down yonder in . . .

It was carnival in New Orleans, and while he sang his heart out he was not in tune with it. And showed it, he knew. Just as Joe Capella's glowering face showed it, just as the rapid turnover of the Carousel's restless customers showed it. Not that most of them, on this orgiastic Tuesday, came to hear much of anything except the sound of their own voices, mingling in drunken glory and incoherence with the hundreds, thousands, of voices, noisemakers and open-door jazz and rock that shake the Quarter to its foundations at carnival. His own lackluster performance couldn't keep even the Crescent Carousel from its destiny of all-night revels. Saying "to hell with it," something like it, he started to drink very early. By midnight, if he still wasn't quite in the swing of it, he was at least lively and loud.

Mardi Gras, Mardi Gras,
Come on down to Mardi Gras.
Grab a gal, grab a guy,
Sing it up, sing it high.
Nothing beams
Like New Orleans
At Mardi Gras.

Mardi Gras . . . Mardi Gras . . .

By one thirty, two, it was one long, loud, seemingly endless community sing—tuneless but triumphant—and even Joe Capella was smiling.

By three he was halfway drunk.

Nothing beams
Like New Orleans . . .

"You weally sing wight, you weally do."

"I do? Thank you."

"Weally wight."

He had noticed her, of course; most of the evening in fact. She was a large, but not obese, woman in her early-to-mid thirties, rather startlingly pretty, almost like a Barbie doll, her long brown eyelashes opening and closing like Barbie's too, mechanically but intriguingly, in time to the music. Her short brown hair was bobbed in the fashion of the twenties, and altogether (despite a Pucci-type pants suit) she seemed of another age and time. The Cupie *w*'s for *r*'s, as well as the old-fashioned Satan mask she fingered but had long since removed, only heightened the illusion.

She had sat at the rotating bar, facing him directly, since the first set. Talking to people on either side of her, of course; particularly if they were men. But her glance never long away from him—his face, his hands on the keys. And drinking as he was, her simple undemanding smile attracted him, so that at some point in the whirling morning hours, between now uncountable sets, he found himself sitting beside her and unthinkingly liking her.

Her name was Baby. Baby Jones. From Ohio. Somewhere.

"Ooh, when you sing it goes wight thwough me. Weally. Honest."

"I preesh . . . *ap*preciate that, thank you."

"Honest. I know all about you too. I do, I weally do. They told me at the Wosevelt Hotel—that's wheah I'm staying?—well, they told me all about you, about how you wuh a well-known wabbi and then up and gave up pweaching for the piano. It's wemahkable, it weally is."

"Vewy. I mean Very."

"But you ah still Jewish? Awen't you?"

"What is 'being Jewish'?"

"Oh . . . I don't know. Just being Jewish I weckon."

"Less . . . *let us* put it this way, as the sages taught. If a palm branch for Sukkuth was acquired by robbery or was withered, it is not valid. If it came from an *asherah* —that's a tree worshiped by idolaters—it is not valid. If its tip was broken off or if its leaves were split, it is not valid. If its leaves were spread apart, it is not valid. Rabbi Judah says: It may be tied up at the end. The thorn-palms of the Oron Mount, near Jerusalem, are valid. A palm-branch three handbreaths in length is valid. If it is long enough to shake."

"Weally? God!"

Way down yonder in . . .

"Bwavo!"

Unlikely, unimaginable, only vaguely remembered: walking beside her through the tired, thinning Quarter streets, dawn a foolish reality; the aftermath of carnival a crazy litter on Canal Street, wondrously tinsely even in light; the Roosevelt Hotel—sleepy, yawning—a Babylonian palace.

Emphasis on *Baby.*

She was soft, she was giving, she was warm, cajoling. She was practiced to perfection. All she wanted—gently, ardently—was "to love you, honey, just love you. To make it and just dwink you dwy." But nothing. Nothing. Even nakedness was defeating. Only the cruel, hallucinatory image of Skip, Slip; touching, holding. And whirlingly—

Jelly, Jelly, what are you . . . ?"

"Billygoat! Lordy, Jack, don't be such a . . ."

"Weeah, honey, just tohn ovuh on yoah weeah . . ."

Baruch Ato Adonoi Elohenu . . .

"I . . . Jelly, I . . ."

"Love. Just love, Jack, love . . ."

"Jacob. Oh God, Jacob, don't feel guilty. Even about . . ."

Mardi Gras, Mardi Gras . . .

"It's horseshit, Jack, just horseshit, Jack . . ."

". . . Echod. Boruch Sh'em Kevod . . ."

"I love you, Jelly, I honestly . . ."

"But just twy, honey, twy. Twy for Baby . . ."

"Billygoat!"

—and at last, sometime in the morning, weary with impotence, he wept like a child between her great breasts, her generous thighs; for some reason; some surface; some depth. Some light.

"It's aw-wight, honey, it's aw-wight. Just sleep. Sleep . . ."

When he waked in the afternoon she was gone. Along with his wallet and watch.

His head and body ached. He was hungry, thirsty, he wanted to vomit, his eyes were both sick and dumb as they roamed about the strange hotel room. He wondered to what other depth he could sink. Still, he had to laugh.

But the season of silliness—his own of self-pity—passed; and life, as they say, went on. He did try to drink less, and managed, after a fashion, to settle into a disciplined routine. He began reading again, avidly, albeit with little or no direction. He couldn't write nor did he attempt to. After a month or so, and so indeliberately that he didn't even think to rationalize it, he began attending Friday night or Saturday morning services at various temples and synagogues about the city, sitting as unobtrusively as possible in the rear of their sanctuaries, neither praying nor feeling the compulsion of prayer, experiencing neither great relief nor great weight, simply letting tradition, or the memory of tradition, absorb him like a long, familiar poem, words accosting not so much mind or heart as some deep recess of the senses, a communion outside God or even himself.

At the Carousel he performed easily and well, if with perfunctory charm, and Joe Capella, smiling broadly at the steady stream of customers, left him alone. Shy came around once or twice, but not to taunt, simply to "chew on the fatty," as he put it.

Sam wrote regularly and persistently, urging him still to Dallas (anywhere but the arms of that trampy *shikse*), letters which he answered only occasionally, with a brief postcard. Thoughtlessly—but so long as she was within distance, somehow not hopelessly—he sang on.

> *. . . Shenandoah*
> *I love your daughter*
> *Away, you rolling river . . .*

It was on a night in late April, toward the end of the last set, that she came in. She was wearing a dark blue, very tailored suit, so conservative for her that it seemed a certainty she was only modeling it, her eyes flashing with secrets she obviously couldn't wait to tell. She sat in a back booth and with child-woman impatience waited. Heart virtually stopped, he made "Impossible Dream" by a breath.

"Hi."

"Hi."

They didn't even order a drink.

"Not the ring thing, not that," she said. Her smile was broad and real. "But let's face it. I'm a miserable sonofabitch without you. We got it the hell and back, darlin, don't we?" Pause as deep and breathless as any in romantic fiction. "So . . ."—more breathless still—"I kicked Slip's ass right out of the sack and dragged my own right back to Jack. How's that for poetry?"

"It's poetry."

"He's boilin wild mad and out for blood. I love you, Jack. Darlin, I do, I do."

It is a sacred thing: the end of loneliness.

CHAPTER EIGHTEEN

"Billygoat! Say you're glad you're back."

"I'm glad I'm back."

"Again. Say it again."

"I'm glad I'm back."

"And that you don't think I'm just a sleep-around chick, no matter what anybody . . ."

"Will I ever figure you out?"

"Don't try, Jack. Don't try, darlin. You know how I feel about One, about Oneness. Most destructive mother ever foisted on us. Fragments, darlin, that's what we are. Fragments, and fragments of fragments, and even . . ."

"All right, I'm resigned. If I *have* to have pretentious philosophy with my . . ."

"Christ, you're laughin, you really are, you're laughin. I love it, laugh again. When you laugh it's to pleasure, it's to pure sweet pleasure. Guys like Slip, when they laugh it's to pain. They don't know it I guess, and couldn't help it if they did, but it's to pain, somehow in takin somethin from you, they hurt . . ."

"Jelly. I don't want to talk about your Slip or Skip or whatever his name is. Any more than I want to talk about . . ."

"You're right. We were just born, a minute ago, and you know what?"

"What?"

"Sammy Beckett said it good. Language is this long sin against the silence that enfolds us."

"You're reading Beckett? Samuel Beckett?"

"Sometimes. Between times."

"Between times? Jelly, what are you trying to . . . ?"

"Between times. You know. Oh, what the shit. Between paintin, darlin, and waitin on tables and . . ."

"And?"

"Fuckin. Is that what you want to hear? *Is that what you want to hear?*"

"Keep your voice down, Jelly, you're . . ."

"Crazy? Sure. Yeah, sure. Oh God—hah, God—I wish everybody was watchin us now. I wish everybody in the whole world was lookin at us now."

"You what?"

"Wish the whole mother world was seein us now. You. Me. I. Naked and movin and touchin and livin. Alive. Alive, like now. Like now. We're beautiful. Did you know that, Jack? We're beautiful. Beautiful. We're so beautiful goddamn beautiful . . ."

"Jelly, you're . . ."

"High? On pot? Dern right I am. High as God. Low as God. High as . . ."

"Black, Jelly, you're drinking it black."

"Billygoat! Take your coffee and . . ."

"*Jelly!*"

"Laugh again, Jack. Laugh again."

"A few sips, Jelly, please, just a . . ."

"He says somethin else too. Sammy Beckett. He says somethin about the ethical yoyo of good and evil . . ."

"Jelly, I love you. Don't, please, whatever it is, I . . ."

"What? You what? Oh hell, Jack, I'm perfectly all right, I just . . . You're sick to your stomach you came back. Ain't you? *Aren't* you?"

"I love you."

"Again. Say it again. Please. Again."

"I love you."

"Oh Jesus! Jack, I . . . Here. How's this? *Shema Yisrael Adonoi Elahena Adonoi Eck* . . . Shit! Let's hear it for Daddy too. Fuck around all you want with heaven, and hell, and even me, so long as you don't . . . I'm sorry, Jack. I really am, I'm very sorry, Jack. I love you, I . . . give a little, take a little . . . let your poor heart break a little . . . that's the story of, that's the glory of . . ."

"More. Drink a little more. That's it. A little more . . ."

"You hate me."

"I love you."

"Bastard. We're driven each other to . . ."

"Yes. I know. Now no more of your pot or whatever you call it, Jelly, no more of . . ."

"Jack. Oh, Jack, Jack, darlin, I . . ."

"Can we sleep now? Just sleep?"

"Are you kiddin? When your beautiful hands are cuppin my bonds for Israel and with just a little more effort are goin to find The American Dream . . ."

"You're not to be believed, Jelly, not to . . ."

"Believe, darlin, believe!"

"I'm not sure I can again, I . . ."

"Jack. Jack! Oh, darlin, when two people are so goddamn beautiful and so goddamn confused . . ."

Morning was a forest of delights.

Night was another part of the forest.

Dream,
When you're feeling . . .

"You was in exceptional form tonight, Reb," Joe Capella said, in the dark early morning, as he was leaving the Carousel; when being back with her, in the crazy pad, was all that mattered. "Makes a difference, right? Between the sheets?"

It was a mild evening, seasonally so, and at the late hour (or early; however you viewed it) Royal Street—street born for people, pleasure—was almost a tomb. Only a stray couple here and there, mostly young, and a few loners, habitués of late night, early morning, peopled the quiet darkness, and these mostly on the far side of Jackson Square, where some hanger-on sound and light still emanated from the French Market. Altogether it was disquietening, and rather sad.

But this was outside him. Inside him there was life and love, spunky twins of anticipation.

He didn't see them until it was too late. There were three of them, that much he saw: all of them tall, muscular, a wall of impenetrable flesh that shot out with lightning precision from the shadows of the Cabildo, pushing him back into them, shadows equally impenetrable, all within the space of a breath. And that one of them was Skip Barry, his bold blondness unmistakable even in shadows. And a soft, tooth-filtered voice: "Sleep with this, Jew!"

Jacob fought back, thought he fought back, but it was all too quick, too overwhelming, really to know. A hundred hands, fists, pummeled virtually every part of him, and within seconds the world went away.

Part Six

CHAPTER NINETEEN

> Thou shalt love the Lord, thy God, With all thy heart, with all thy soul, and with all thy might. And these words, which I command thee this day, shall be upon thy heart. Thou shalt . . .

"Hey, Miss, stop, you can't go in there . . ."

"Get out of my way, you friggin . . ."

"Lady, please, the man's . . ."

"Alive. Alive! Say he's . . ."

". . . hurt, hurt bad, real bad, but he's . . ."

". . . left arm, both legs, four ribs, concussion . . ."

"Lung . . ."

"Christ!"

". . . as soon as we get blood. We'll operate as soon as we get . . ."

"Jack? Jack darlin . . . ?"

"Miss, please . . ."

"I'm Sam."

"Sam?"

"His brother."

"Oh. Oh yeah . . ."

"And this is my wife. Esther, this is . . ."

"I won't stay in the same room with such a . . ."

"Esther, this is no time . . ."

"I said I will not, absolutely will not . . ."

"Blow it out your . . ."

"We shouldn't have come. Sam, I knew we shouldn't have . . ."

". . . home with us, we'll take him to Dallas . . ."

"Billygoat! He'll do whatever he damn well . . ."

"Slut!"

"Why, you phony farcical piece of . . ."

". . . blood. He's lost an inordinate amount of . . ."

". . . weeks, months . . ."

". . . rest, quiet . . ."

"Boruch Ato Adonoi . . ."

"Jack, darlin, I love you, but any more of that foxhole crap . . ."

In late summer, when the sun is at its most intense—when water meets sky in blinding green-white continuum—the Mississippi Gulf Coast is a popular playground for the active, the young. By day there is sailing, power boating, salt-water or fresh-water fishing, horseback riding, golf, swimming in artisian pools or from the wondrous white beaches. By night, if you are up to it, there is flounder gigging by lantern, and drinking, eating, dancing, laughing. Loving. Killing time, forgetting time, cherishing time, renouncing time. From Bay St. Louis to Biloxi—

from romantic old homes and gardens (Jefferson Davis's *Beauvoir* and Woodrow Wilson's Winter White House among them) to the most modern hotels and motels, nightclubs and restaurants—there are twenty-six pleasure-filled miles in the lands and waters of the Chinchuba, Biloxi, Chapitoulas, and Chaouacha Indians. For the young, the active.

For the inactive—the old, the aging, the lame, the recuperative—there are, of course, the good long hours of salt air and sun. Particularly at Pass Christian, between Bay St. Louis and Gulfport, where life is quieter, softer, more reflective.

We got to do, man, do
We got to be, man, be
We got to go, man, go
We got to love, man, love
We got to feel, man, feel
We got to . . .

"If they don't turn off the phonograph at that awful place next door I'm gonna scream," said the woman.

"Lousy kids takin over every decent place left," said the man.

"That's what happens when you forsake God and country for drugs and sex," said the other woman.

"Dern tootin it is," said the other man.

Jacob heard, didn't hear. Their voices, from the other end of the deck of the Sea Gull Haven, mingled uncertainly with the gentler breaking of waves on the beach below. Even the loud, defiant music from the deck of the Beachcomber across the way failed to penetrate him. He was far too lost in the sun, in thoughts seared by the sun, to be more than vaguely aware of sound outside them.

It was hot, strenuously hot—infinitely welcome. Jacob was responding to it as a lover in half-sleep. His body, healing slowly but surely, was absorbent. It was good; beautiful, good. After interminable weeks in the hospital —interminable weeks of bewilderment and pain, of Sam and Esther—the sea air was more than balm; it was blessing.

He had lived. There were times, particularly after the two operations (one of his lungs had been damaged; there had been severe internal hemorrhage) when even that distinction had been doubtful. But he had lived. However much he would carry with him the rest of his life the scars of it. And the limp, the large labored limp—

"The foot itself was too badly mangled, we had to do it. It must have gotten twisted between iron rails or something, it was so . . . But what the hell? We have artificial devices now you couldn't have imagined even five years ago. Why, in time no one will even notice it, much less . . . Hell, man you should thank God every day you're even . . ."

—living.

"Don't leave me, Jelly."

"Leave you? Who the hell said anything about leavin you? As long as that face and that brain and those arms, not to mention those adorable private parts, are all in workin order, darlin, I'm your true devoted chick, your slave woman, your . . ."

"Marry me, Jelly."

"Unh-unh. I'll live with you, Jack, I'll love you, Jack, but some old bastard's blessin? Not for me, Jack. Not for us. Not for all the tea in . . ."

"The land of milk and honey?"

He broke from his reverie with a half-startled squint at the sun, slowing bringing into focus the glistening brown blondeness of her, tall and proud, standing beside his deck chaise with half an eye (of both amusement and defiance) on the other sunning guests on the deck of the Sea Gull Haven, who never failed to look with curiosity, bewilderment, or disapproval on the man with the blanket over his legs, even at blazing noon, and the girl whose bikini covered less.

"The land of what?" he said, reaching for her hand.

"Milk and honey," she said, pulling a deck chair up beside him. "That's Hebrew for dreamland."

"I see."

He leaned over lightly to kiss her. She responded, but not lightly. There was an audible sigh (gasp) from the two middle-aged couples at the other end of the deck.

Jelly laughed. "A rest home is right. But you needed it. *We* needed it. Nice old comfy middle class. And you're gettin too much sun, you're red as a robin."

"Robin?"

"Rooster. Rooster, robin, lobster, beet. What the hell. You've been out here too long, you better go inside."

"Yes, Mother."

"*Baruch Ato Adonoi* to you too. See, I'm learnin." She stretched luxuriantly. The unself-consciousness of it was almost heartbreaking. "Ooh, this sun, this sweet Satan sun."

He laughed. "You'd say anything for the sake of alliteration, wouldn't you? Whether it means anything or not."

"Anything," she laughed too. "Anything, anything, anything. And you look healthy as a horse right now so why don't we both go inside and settle ourselves down to a nice long . . ."

"A few minutes more," he said, stretching too. "It's so great out here. Even copulation, if you'll pardon the expression, can't compete."

She touched his arm; stroked it. Said softly, "Enjoy, darlin. Smartass."

She walked (if a tall gazelle can be said to walk) to the railing; smiling. "The ocean's a great leveler," she said; turning to him. "It's like being born and dyin at the same time." The silence around them, the silly song from the Beachcomber—*Dreamin it ain't doin' it*—obviated by their absorption in themselves.

"Place is really rundown," said the woman.

"Not like it used to be," said the man.

"Wonder they don't take niggers," said the other woman.

"Don't be too sure they don't," said the other man.

The music from the Beachcomber broke through.

Yeh Yeh Yeh
You got to Yeh Yeh Yeh . . .

"I'm gonna scream," said the woman.

"Oughta bomb 'em, every last one of 'em." said the man.

"I talked to Shy this mornin," said Jelly. "Honestly, I think that cat's dandruff comes from his brain. Smokin pot and drinkin Drambuie at the same time. And at this hour."

"Shy?" he said. "You called Shy? In New Orleans?"

"No, in Transylvania. Silly! Of course, New Orleans."

"Why?"

"You know why."

"Jelly," he said, sitting up, "I thought we'd agreed . . ."

"They still haven't found him. Any of them. Boy! When

I named him 'Slip' I was downright prophetic. He's slipped through every net you can . . ."

"Jelly, forget it. Please. It doesn't matter. Not any more. It doesn't matter."

"It matters. To me it matters." Her hands on the railing were hard, and for a moment her face was a match for them. "If ever I wanted to see somebody literally hang by his balls . . ."

Jacob laid back down. "Look," he said, "over by the pier. The gulls are marvels today. They're really fascinating, you know. They have a life style that's almost musical, it's so . . ."

She eased too. "Darlin, I wasn't kiddin, you *are* gettin too much sun. At least put a shirt on . . ."

He laughed, shaking his head. "My fate," he said. "Condemned forever to the skirts of a Jewish mother."

She smiled. "I love you, Jack," she said.

He closed his eyes. "It's your nature to love cripples."

"Go fuck yourself."

The days passed in a kind of gauzelike perfection, aimless but full, as sure as they were swift. When he was able they went deep-sea fishing for whole days and rode horseback through thick pine woods and drove to seashore restaurants from Gulfport to Biloxi and, because he wouldn't yet venture to swim, bathed in each other's delight. If it was still a time of fresh pain it was also a time of fresh pleasure. August slipped into September like a daydream.

CHAPTER TWENTY

On the twentieth of October he began playing piano and singing in the new Sazerac Room of the Roosevelt Hotel, and on the ninth of December Jelly announced that she was pregnant.

Wait till you see her . . .

In his own way, at his new stand, from the very first night, Jack White was an even larger success than he had been at the Crescent Carousel. "The old crows," said Jelly, "may like to hear you sing, but they *love* to see you limp."

He had taken the job, not only because they wanted to remain in New Orleans, but because the Carousel had closed its doors. "Sorry, Reb," Joe Capella had said, "but I thought you was a goner. And you was the draw, let's face it. So you'll go on to bigger things. Me? I'll wind up with a contract from *Cosa Nostra*. If I'm lucky."

The Sazerac Room, with its expensive antebellum plantation decor and its appeal not only to hotel guests but the "beautiful people" of New Orleans, signaled a new and somewhat discomfiting direction in Jacob's professional life. He had moved uptown. He was reviewed in both the *Times Picayune* and *States Item*—"downright reverently," his new employer, Jerry Schwartz, beamed ethnically all round. He was established, so to speak, as a New Orleans celebrity of the first rank, and being stopped on Canal Street to sign autographs became almost commonplace.

"Wouldn't you know," laughed Jelly. "You can take the cat out of the Establishment but you can't take the Establishment out of the cat. Ashes to ashes and . . ."

Their personal lives changed too. Although they remained in the St. Peter Street apartment, Jelly gave up her job at the Rue de la Pay—"No ring, darlin, but squatter's rights"—and began painting like a fiend. He himself no longer wrote, or made any attempt to, and the uncertain safaris to synagogues were now the sprain of a wounded past. They both, however, poured themselves into off-hours labor for the League of Human Betterment, and somehow it gave strength to time; it sufficed.

His own strength returned remarkably, he gained weight, flourished.

Sunrise,
Sunset . . .

It was after midnight, the Sazerac Room was still crowded and boisterous, when she came in and at a dark back table told him about the baby.

"We're goin to 'ave a little strahnger, as the sayin goes. Bless your seed, darlin, as the sayin . . ."

"You *have* to marry me now," he said.

"Billygoat," she said. "Love babies, otherwise known as bastards, are the hope of the future."

"Be practical for once in your life, Jelly. We do have a responsibility no matter what . . ."

"I hope he opts for life," she said. "I just hope the little shithead opts for life."

"It's essential we marry, Jelly," he said.

"It's essential I get my sexy body back in shape," she said. "So will you just let me get through these inevitable months without undue emotional stress? Thank you, Daddy. Boy! Talk about the ladies' day door prize!"

There was nothing for him but to smile.

"I hear they live together in sin," said the woman.

"No shit," said the man.

During the Christmas season, Shy and his roommate, Andrew P. Gatesworth, gave a party for them, "to celebrate"—as the latter so archly put it—"the fragile cord between near-death and near-birth." By any standard, it was a smashing affair.

Most of those who were there were friends or acquaintances of Shy or Andrew P. or Jelly, all Quarter-located or Quarter-oriented, all committed—in one way or another—if not to subterranean life, at least to an island one. They talked a great deal of America—of the black in America, the Establishment in America, provincialism in America—but they were clearly unconcerned with America. They were concerned—and in their intense emotion, oddly unemotionally—simply with enjoyment or escape, if the two are indeed separable. They were gypsies, very physical gypsies, and while the world outside the Quarter was not to be denied, it was really vague and undefined. Who was who and who was what, who was gay and who was straight—within the confines of a dozen narrow secret streets—this was The World.

Still, they were cheerful, and in the banshee-baroque setting of Andrew P.'s apartment (Jelly's description of the indescribable assemblage of Victorian and neo-African atrocities) even amusing. Particularly after several drinks and with Jelly's radiance all around him, like the sun at night.

"Havin a good time, darlin?"—sometime in the night, linking an arm with his; breaking up a cul de sac with a girl with long brown hair and a man with a long brown beard who lived together and had had two children together—"without benefit of the cotton-pickin clergy, man, you oughta know"; drunken kinship—and who questioned incoherently "that sundown-to-sundown stuff of the Jewish religion when today's meteorologists . . ."

"I'm fine," he said.

"Mad party isn't it?" she said.

"Mad," said the girl.

"Really mad," said the guy.

And it was.

Andrew P.—"Please call me Andy, honey"—tried for him in the kitchen. A bosomy landlady who had once controlled the Court of the Two Sisters tried a turn on his way to the bathroom. Even Shy—drunk and incongruously despondent—made a pass in the hall.

"Fame and fortune," laughed Jelly. "Get me the hell out of here, Jack. I'm a lady with child."

But somehow the party, inconsequential in itself, marked a new direction in their social lives. They began seeing people together, something they had not done before, meeting for dinner, even having them at the apartment. And at Quarter parties, having "Jack and Jelly" became a thing. In all, the months of her pregnancy were the most satisfying he had ever known.

It tormented him, of course, that she remained adamant about marriage, even as her belly expanded. But somehow that too was eased by her nearness—her spirit, her laughter, her utter unpredictability. By the nights, the mornings, when in uncomplicated nakedness they touched one another: he stroking the lovely swelling of her (she was carrying large); she caressing and finally healing his many scars.

"See, darlin? Guilt is for the really guilty, not the innocent. We're the innocent, darlin. We're the beautiful fuckin innocent."

A way of life.

The baby, a boy, was born in May. He weighed eleven pounds.

They gave a great deal of thought to naming him. Her own father, of course, was completely estranged, not that "Josephus" seriously entered their minds. And she was uncompromising when it came to Biblical names. In the end they named him William ("The Conqueror").

Billy.

Billy White.

CHAPTER TWENTY-ONE

Rabbi Nahman of Bratzlav says: "God does not do the same thing twice." That which is, is single and for once. It plunges out of the flood of returns, new and never having happened before. Each person is a new thing in the world.

Often in the weeks following the birth of his son, Jacob found himself reading again. The Hasidic doctrines and stories in particular drew him. And in his great joy and great guilt he dared not ask himself why.

The baby was a banquet. "A feast, a little feast," Jelly laughed, cried; kissing, love-biting, chunks from him. "And ours, Jack, ours, ours. Oh, you'll have your hangups, Billy boy. You'll have your billygoat hangups. But please something, *somebody*, they won't be your mama's and they won't be your daddy's and they won't be . . ."

Rabbi Moshe Leib of Sasov once gave his last coin to a man of evil reputation. His students reproached him for it.

Whereupon he replied: "Shall I be more particular than God, who gave the coin to me?"

He was a good baby. He laughed (gurgled) a great deal. He had a strong grip on one's finger, a strong expression of pain or pleasure on his face. He was Someone.

Someone.

A young man was asked by Rabbi Yitzhak Meir of Ger if he had learned Torah. "Just a little," replied the youth. "That is all anyone ever has learned of the Torah," said the rabbi.

"Jelly, we're going to get married," he said. "Today, tomorrow, the day after. No later. Now. *Now*. We have a child, we . . . we just can't . . ."

"What? Just can't what? Billygoat! Darlin, we've made it, we have heaven and earth, we're home free, free, *he's* free, *Billy's* free . . ."

"I mean it, Jelly. I've never meant anything more in my . . ."

"I know, darlin, I know. And we'll talk about it. I reckon we'll have to talk about it. But for now, Jack . . . darlin . . . 'literation or no 'literation . . . will you please just go sing your swinging songs at the Sazerac . . ."

The bells are ringing
For me and my . . .

CHAPTER TWENTY-TWO

Raindrops keep falling on my . . .

It was a noisy Fourth of July eve. The Sazerac Room was mobbed and oiled.

Well oiled.

" 'Star Spangled Banner,' Jack!"

" 'My Country 'Tis of Thee,' Jack!"

" 'America the Beautiful,' Jack!"

" 'Deep in the Heart of Texas,' Jack!"

" 'Ooh Mama, Ooh Mama . . .' "

It was not a night for the love songs of Jack White. At two, exhausted, he was glad to call it a night.

Canal Street and the Quarter were raucous still. The young mainly, stars and stripes across their breasts and behinds, the Spirit of '76 born again in their pot-high voices.

"Hey, Ex!"

"Up the flagpole, Ex!"

"Up the Vietnamese, Ex!"

"Up the Israelis, Ex!"

"Hey . . . nobody meant nothin personal, Ex . . ."

It was a warm night as well; muggy. The river fog was very thick. Mosquitos, en masse, danced a bead curtain at every corner. Singing, stinging, in equal celebration.

Lights were on in the apartment. The baby, he thought; the baby was fretful.

"I've sat it out," said Sam. "Been here four hours. He's a beautiful child, Jacob."

Jacob stood almost dumbly in the room's bright glare, the weight of him on his good leg both heavy and uncomfortable. His brother sat in a corner chair half eclipsed by scattered books and canvases, a stern smile on his wide face. Jelly, in devastating pink silk leotards, tight as sin, was sprawled in self-effacing mockery on the magazine-littered sofa. Her eyes were slightly glazed. Had she been with Shy again, he wondered. Grass again? After she'd promised? . . . The whole scene had the look of a berserk stagehand's whimsy.

Jacob took a chair across from his brother, stacking its burden of League for Human Betterment pamphlets on the floor. "I had no idea you were coming," he said.

Sam Weiss, without changing expression, replied, "I know."

"Is Esther with you?"

"She stayed in Dallas. She has to get the children ready for camp."

"I see. And how are they? The children?"

"They're fine. Fine."

Jelly laughed; a high, deliberately wanton, note. "I'm surprised he didn't say 'swell.' "

Sam stiffened visibly. But his smile, while hardening

even more, remained fixed. "I don't think we've had . . . mmn . . . the clearest communication these past couple of hours," he said.

She laughed again. "You can sure as shit bank your money there, Buster."

Jacob looked restively about him. "Don't you want a drink, Sam? Coffee?"

"Nothing, thanks."

The silence from the peopleless street below was deafening. But there was another presence in the room, loud and dismaying. Jacob breathed deeply while his brother lit a cigarette.

"You're recovered completely now, Jacob?" he asked.

"Yes, I think. All things considered."

"Good. That's good."

Jacob had not felt real pain in the leg of his severed foot for some time. It was there now, and very real.

"Are you sure you don't want a drink?" he said.

"No, no drink."

"I think I'll get one."

"Better you should get a psychiatrist."

Jelly fixed him the drink. Her smile was warm even as vestiges of anger and resentment laced it.

"Billy sleeping soundly?" he asked, as she handed him the glass.

"Like a soldier," she said; slurred. "A real little soldier."

Even Sam winced.

Jacob sighed. "All right," he said. "What grievous sin has brought us all together this time?" As if he didn't know.

Jelly laughed again; if anything, more harshly. "Let Mister Super Respectable Salami spread it on," she said. "He's the big mouthful tonight."

Jacob paled ."Jelly, there's one thing I absolutely won't . . ."

But Sam was on his feet. "It's all right, Jacob, anti-Semitism right now I expect. She's upset."

"*Upset?* Billygoat! Baby, you can kiss my ass from here to . . ."

"Please, Miss."

"*Miss?*"

"Is there any other way to address you?"

"Why, you goddamn butcherin . . ."

"This isn't necessary. You'll wake the baby."

"*He's my baby!*"

Who slept soundly through it all, the little soldier. Jacob pulled himself wearily from the chair and limped (very perceptibly, he knew) to the kitchen for another drink. Empty formula bottles, diapers, all of the paraphernalia of a baby, were everywhere. The smell of a baby—sweet, sour, deep—was everywhere too. He dawdled over the drink as long as he could but Jelly's voice from the living room—while low, waspish—was impossible to ignore.

"You can make all the threats you want, Mister, it's not *your* life or *your* baby. And you just happen to be in a home—a goddamn beautiful home—which your craven sensibilities couldn't absorb in a million years . . . where there's life and love and fun—yes, *fun* . . ."

And Sam's—equally low but strong—impossible to escape.

"Yes, I can see. If your idea of home is a pigsty . . ."

Jacob paced himself slowly back to them. "What is it you want, Sam?" he asked.

His brother, in awkward gesture, looked genuinely moved and pained. "Jacob," he said, taking his seat again, brushing an imaginary spot from his obviously new and expensive jacket, "we all know—that is, we all feel, we sympathize, we—well, God knows you've been through . . ."

"What is it you want, Sam?"

Jelly, in an inimitable upright bolt, legs folded under her like secret weapons, smashed through the communications barrier like a tigress. "He wants Billy. Says he'll take it to court. That is, if we're not married. He wants decency and piety and respect for the law, he wants the sanctity of centuries, the good blind toll of time. The silly-ass soul-suckin shit of time. Actually, what he wants is to get a little peace from his wife's big fuckin mouth."

"Jelly!"

"It's true. Oh what the hell, Jack, it's true and you know it."

Sam shifted with all the grace of a walrus in his shabby chair. "This is still the South," he said quietly. "Even overlooking moral considerations, the courts down here . . ."

"Billygoat! I'm a mother, baby! And I mean that in more ways than one!"

Jacob shifted too. "I don't believe this is your concern, Sam," he said. "Oh, concern perhaps. But not responsibility. Jelly and I are quite capable of working out our own situation."

"*Situation?*" She came within an octave of screaming. "*What* situation? Jack, there's no reason for this, no reason for . . ."

"There's plenty of reason," said Sam, his face now flushed and almost formidably full. "I'm sorry. I don't find this crazy childish rebellion very funny, much less healthy. Especially in a middle-aged man, a man who was ordained, ordained in the name of God, a spiritual leader, a Jew, a father . . ."

"Billygoat!"—laughter soft, oddly lovely, almost a child's —"I'll bet you've never done it dog-fashion while you were recitin 'Sonnets from the Portuguese.' And had a fine beautiful baby to give soul to it, fire . . ."

"Now, listen, Miss, I've had about all I can take from you . . ."

"Dallas ain't but a dream away."

". . . I'll have the law down so fast . . ."

"No shit?"

". . . and if you think I'm shittin . . ."

Her laughter, or so it seemed, was demonic. The whole room, the whole world, was demonic. The whole . . .

Raindrops keep falling on my . . .

The night's song, in a thousand offkey voices, coursed through him. Shakily, he rose. "I'm very tired tonight, Sam," he said. "We'll talk tomorrow. At the hotel or somewhere. All right?"

His brother rose too, flushed still, anger uneasily suppressed. "Tomorrow don't wash away today," he said. Pausing, somewhat imperiously, at the door. "You got a lot of filth in your life, Jacob. An awful lot of filth."

Even in the late hour Jacob sat down again with his drink, and within seconds Jelly was on the floor beside him, embracing his good leg with protective fierceness.

"We cheat and steal and hate in the light, Jack. And then have to love in the dark."

Stroking her hair, that infinite hair, he said—choked—"You know that deep inside I feel the same thing as Sam does, Jelly. About marriage, about . . ."

The baby, who had slept through it all, cried like the damned from their bedroom. In less than a moment he was in her arms, and held as fiercely, as protectively, as had been his own good leg.

"Yes, Billy boy, when you grow big and strong and up to your ass with all that external God crap, there'll be . . ."

They were married in September; quietly, by a justice of the peace on Bienville. Shy and Andrew P. were witnesses.

"Here's to compromise," she said. "And love. Yes, love, darlin. I hope to hell I forgive myself. Forgive you. I hope to hell we forgive ourselves. And just go on. You and me and Billy. And that we can still laugh and cry and make love and say Screw 'em. Screw 'em all."

Neither laughing nor crying.

CHAPTER TWENTY-THREE

"Whooee! We got us a boy heah, man. We got us a real fine sluggin boy heah!"

Shy, backing away in mock terror from Billy's twenty-month-old punches, was grinning broadly.

"Mole, mole," the boy was screaming ecstatically. "Mole, mole." More, more.

"Mole off to bed, that where you mole," the new housekeeper, Sugaree, laughed, sweeping the child into her big brown arms. Originally from Barbados, she had been a dishwasher at the Rue de la Pay, and a friend to Jelly. She was very fat and content.

"Day, day," the boy cried, arms dramatically spread. Daddy, daddy. In the evolution of vocabulary it had become the child's name for him.

Jacob, automatically, started to rise, reach out, but Sugaree's authoratitive frown sat him back down.

"Day! Day!"

"Off we go. Off to Sugareeland."

Even in frustration, fury, he was blond and bold and beautiful.

When they were gone Shy said, "Shit, man. Shee-ut. You got it made."

"Yes," he smiled; vaguely. "Made."

"Yessir. Made. Hogwallowed made." Looking around again at the spacious Pastillon apartment with its high ceilings and tall windows, its polished century-old floors, its eighteenth-century-Spanish furniture, so massively graceful; its soft ivory walls. "And there's nobody deserves it more than you, Jack. Nobody."

"Thank you, Shy."

"Great new pad, great little old boy, great . . . No sir, nobody. But nobody. And I got to haul butt to work." Stretching, he reached to a chair for his topcoat. It was early January and exceptionally cold out. "Tell old Jelly I'm sorry I missed seein her, you heah?" Jelly had gotten a part in Le Petit Theatre's production of *The Crucible,* and was rehearsing.

"Of course," said Jacob. "Thank you for coming over, Shy."

"Hell, man, no call for thankin. I got to experience envy once in a while, too, you know."

When he was gone, when Billy's loud protests in the back room had trailed into sleep and Sugaree had retired to her own room, Jacob picked up the Von Weizsacker book he had been reading earlier, and taking a chair (an imitation leather recliner, the only real incongruity in the room) by one of the windows overlooking Jackson Square, resumed; tried to resume—

Seen with external objectivity, original suffering and original guilt are age-old biological facts. All beings fight the fight for life. All must suffer and die, all must cause suffering and much ill. Subjectively, however, their suffering is less than that of man in proportion to their lesser sensitivity and, above all, their lesser vision of past and future. Man is essentially the suffering being. Man alone bears attributable guilt. But in man's suffering and in his guilt we grow aware of what objectively was there even before. It says in the story of man's fall: "And Adam and Eve saw that they were naked, and they were ashamed." Man is the being who shudders at his own nakedness.

The shudder would be senseless if man did not feel within himself the possibility of a goodness beyond that of instinct, the goodness of insight. And even as the shudder also reflects

—but neither mind nor heart were in it. Restively, he tossed it aside. Sundays, the nights off, were untenable. Particularly since Jelly had become involved in Little Theatre.

For a moment his face, although physically he wasn't aware of it, was ice. A frown skated across it. Carrying in its brief passage some sixteen months of his second marriage.

"I feel different. I really do, I feel different."

"Nothing's different, Jelly. We're simply legal."

"That's why I feel different."

"My darling darling bride."

"Darlin bride my ass. Say 'whore' and you might get more positive reaction."

"Don't ever grow up. Jelly, don't ever grow up."

"Well, at least you're laughin. At least that. If bein able to feel morally priggish . . ."

"Come here."

" .. . and all so puffy and proper . . ."

"I said come here."

"Boy! Do tables turn. Maybe that's what's different. Before I got this silly ring it was *me* couldn't get enough of *you*."

"You don't mean that."

" 'Course not. Mr. and Mrs. to hell, darlin, I don't think we'll ever get enough of each other."

But from those first days it *had* been different. Not in any large, really definable way, simply in gestures, a look away, a small silence. Enlarging gradually, imperceptibly, into a new kind of freedom with each other, a freedom more careless and so more petty, the kind of freedom that only possession, or the sanction of possession, can impose. A freedom in which one another's virtues are a little less amusing and the faults a little more visible.

"Jelly, can't you clean this place up, just once in awhile . . . ?"

"Jack, can't you get away from those dreadful old books, read a racy novel or somethin . . . just once in a . . . ?"

In bed, of course—that ageless tranquilizer—they were as well met as ever, bodies responding to each other, rewarding each other, with a fierceness and gentleness that transcended all of it. And there was Billy—mewling, puking, beautiful Billy.

He became—"as is just too commonplace and maudlin to even talk about," said Jelly—the center of their lives. Jacob found himself impatient to leave the Sazerac Room in the dark early mornings, to look upon the child asleep in his crib in their bedroom, to smile upon the noisy faces made in sleep. Mornings, he waked to the infinite delight of him, fresh with the smell and vigor of day. Jelly, in her own childlike pleasure, practically made a cult of him, holding him (though she would never know it) as one holds a sacred religious object: an icon—or a Torah. Or so the path of his imagination in the first feverish months of fatherhood.

Still . . .

"Where did the fun go, Jack?"

"The what?"

"The fun."

"Jelly, don't be absurd."

"Jelly, don't be absurd. See? I can imitate you to a tee. You know exactly what I mean. The fun. *Fun.*"

"You're using the word 'fun' a great deal lately. It used to be 'joy.' "

"All right then, joy. Joy! I can't even say 'fuck' now without throwin up."

"If you'll excuse the rhyme, that's *growing* up."

"Fuck!"

"Fun?"

"No. Oh, Jack . . . darlin . . . darlin Jack . . . Help me. Don't make light of me. Help me."

"Help you what, Jelly?"

"I don't know. Help me to . . . somethin. Oh Billygoat, I don't know, just . . . somethin."

"You asked me that a long time ago. Remember?"

"Asked you what?"

"To help you."

"I did?"

"And didn't mean a word of it. Now, kiss me good night. Or good morning. Whichever it is."

"I wish we wasn't married."

"Weren't."

"I don't feel playful about all this, so don't push it."

"I love you, Jelly. I love Billy. I love *us*. What else is there to . . . ?"

"*Mrs.* White. Or Weiss. Or whatever the hell we are. I just wish we were . . ."

"We are. We are, baby."

"That's the first time you ever called me that."

"Called you what?"

"Baby. That or anything except Jelly."

"I never realized."

"Marriage ain't for eagles. And don't say *isn't.*"

"I didn't say *isn't.*"

"Or for seagulls or for . . ."

"Or for what, Jelly? Here, move here, I . . ."

"Sandpipers. Herons. It doesn't matter. Any bird that preys. Any bird that . . . Oh, I don't know. That has to eat to survive, I guess."

"We all have to eat to survive, Jelly."

"*But not like this!*"

"Jelly . . . what is it you . . . ?"

"I have to piss."

"Jelly, that's not very funny, I . . ."

"What? You what? Oh, Jack, for Christsake we're . . . *Shema Yisrael Adonoi El—*"

"It's all I can do not to hit you."

"Good. Now there's fun. Joy . . ."

"What is it you want, Jelly?"

"Nothin. To be free. To be bound but free. Is that a lot?"

"Oh for the love of . . ."

"Christ. But then you never believed in Christ, did you. Well, then, for the love of . . ."

"What is it you want, Jelly? What is it you ever wanted?"

"I don't know. Anything but what I had I guess."
"Had? Or have?"
"Oh, go . . ."

. . . ringing
For me and my . . .

". . . time, Jack. There was a time when without all this shit—shee-utt, as Shy would say—when we . . ."
"You have to start painting more, Jelly. You need . . ."
"Billygoat! I need, you need, we need . . ."
"Billy needs changing."
"*I know my own child!*"
"Jelly . . . baby—yes, *baby*—why are we . . .?"
"I don't know. Maybe the truth is you're still a rabbi, or at least an uptight Jew, and I'm still a . . ."

Not that it was inevitable, but the St. Peter apartment grew too small. "The very thought of leavin this beautiful little hutch bends my mind," she said, but they began looking for larger quarters nonetheless. About one thing she was unshakable: they would never leave the Quarter. "My baby's goin to grow up breathin life, not gaspin for it."

The Pastillon vacancy (rare and much sought after; the long red brick building overlooking Jackson Square, completed in 1850, was said to be one of the first apartment houses in the United States, occupied well into the twentieth century by the city's fashionable set. The Baroness Pastillon herself lived in one of them, where she entertained Jenny Lind in 1851. The family initials, *AP*—for Aupert and Pastillon—woven so gracefully through the balcony iron work, are a highlight of sight-seeing tours)—the great old building's vacancy signaled yet another change in their lives.

"I have to have it, Jack. I absolutely have to have it."

"But, Jelly, it's so large, you couldn't possibly keep it up."

"I couldn't? My, my. I guess you're sittin there just dyin to tell me what a slob I am."

"Oh for the love of . . . Who said anything about . . . ?"

"You know that's what you meant, darlin, so don't look so friggin innocent. I'm sure you wish it was *her* keepin everything so nice and clean and antiseptic."

"Her? Jelly, what are you . . . ?"

"Her. *Her.* Puny Mrs. Rabbi . . ."

"You really are a bitch, you know that?"

"Your sweet ass I know that! And I know somethin else too. You're about as free of the goddamn past as . . . Oh, Jack, Jack, darlin, forgive me, it's just that it's all so . . . I love you, Jack. Christ only knows how much I love you."

"And I you, Jelly. I you. Whatever we say or do or . . ."

"Jack. Jack, this is Sugaree. Sugaree, Jack. She's goin to live with us. What the hell. Liverwurst and love songs can afford her. We might as well put all that Establishment bread into clean floors."

And the woman *had* been a godsend. Billy adored her and the new place was immaculate.

Still . . .

"I'm goin out of my tree, darlin, I really am. Billy, the paintin, they're only so much, I . . . Jack, there are these cats at Le Petit doin that Arthur Miller thing, you know, *The Crucible* . . . and they want me to read for it. Can you imagine it? Me actin? But then why the hell not. When you've been actin all your life . . ."

He started going, albeit irregularly, to temples and synagogues again, not daring to ask himself why. Tradition, like the giant predatory crab that it is, simply enfolded him. *On this day, holy unto Israel, we enter this sanctuary to unite with our brethren in worship. We come unto Thee, O God, with joyous gratitude for the strength Thou hast given us to do our work in the past week, and for the fortitude to meet trials and temptations. May this hour of devotion . . .*

He drank a great deal one day and, with small ceremony, in the office of the Orleans Parish clerk, had the name of his son changed to William Weiss.

"The fun, Jack, the fun. Where the fuck did the fun go?"

"Day? Day?"

Startled, he looked up. The boy, still three-quarters in sleep, in Sugareeland, weaved shakily beside him.

"Billy?"—in spite of himself, smiling—"What are you doing out of bed? You should be long asleep."

"Sweep."

Jacob scooped him up, and planting him securely at the base of his good leg, holding him against him with outrageous strength, or love, sang him back to sleep.

Christopher Robin
Is counting his sheep . . .

Staring the while at the lone painting on the facing wall, one of Jelly's recent watercolors, a very original but crudely executed fantasy of sexual intercourse at the gates of heaven.

CHAPTER TWENTY-FOUR

"It a full moon out," said Sugaree. "That mean, for some, no sleep tonight. For them that know its dark side, no bloody sleep tonight."

Jelly laughed. "I'm skittish enough right now without all your voodoo, darlin. Now pop off and give Billy his bath."

It was opening night of *The Crucible* and the apartment was electric with it. Jelly had run about like a wild fawn all day, with Sugaree a blind opossum behind her. Even Billy had been affected, laughing and crying with equal uncertainty. Jacob himself had taken the evening off, at least until midnight, promising vaguely to go in for the late sets.

"Boy! For a silly amateur production . . ."

He had sent her a telegram, in care of the theater, which was delivered to the apartment by mistake. *Break a leg. But keep a foot.* Which catapulted the household into total hysteria.

"Day! Day!" the boy screamed when they left.

"I think he loves you more than he does me," she said.

"I saw Goody Osburn with the Devil!"
"I saw Goody Howe with the Devil!"
"I saw Martha Bellows . . ."
". . . Goody Sibber . . ."
". . . Alice Barrow . . ."
"I saw Goody Hawkins with the Devil!"
". . . Goody Bibber . . ."
". . . Goody Booth . . ."

It was a remarkably successful performance, several cuts above the usual Little Theater production. Jelly, in the role of one of the hysterical Salem girls, was an unmistakable presence. Afterward, in a striking new pants suit, she literally glowed with it.

The cast-and-crew party was held at the Garden District home of a Mrs. Dominique Pierre-Travaille, one of Le Petit's wealthier patrons. It was a lavish house and a lavish party and the large assembly, already drunk with themselves, was plastered in less than an hour, Jelly the most flamboyantly of all.

"I saw Goody Sibber, Goody Bibber, Goody Booth"—wildly, meaninglessly, the way Billy made mighty sounds; as if, having become suddenly aware of one's lungs, one had no choice but to ride them out. But she was infectious, and almost the entire company (with whom she obviously had large rapport) responded in kind. Giddy Goody laughter shook the foundation of Mrs. Dominique Pierre-Travaille's legendary structure.

"They are little children, our creative ones," his hostess, a very thin, rather bonily aristocratic woman in her early sixties, said to him in some antique-laden corner at some point in time around midnight. "Is this not so, Rabbi? Or does one still address you as Rabbi?" But Jacob only vaguely heard her. His ears, like his eyes, were channeled solely on Jelly, who on a French Provincial loveseat was leaning both sloppily and determinedly against one of the actors in the play, a handsome dark-skinned youth with a mane of coal-black hair, openly, but not obviously, half Negro. Nor was it Jacob's imagination that she was stroking the upper parts of his legs.

"Excuse me," he said to Mrs. Pierre-Travaille, whose silent nod showed that she hadn't missed very much of it either.

"Jelly, I promised Jerry I'd come in for the late sets. Why don't you get your coat? You can have a nightcap there."

"Billygoat! We just got here!" Her pout was less playful than defiant.

"Jelly, I . . . I'd like . . ." He was stammering, actually stammering.

"You run on, darlin, and sing dreamy for the dames. Tonight's Mrs.'s night. Mizzezes. I like that. Mizzezes. Don't worry 'bout me for Christ sake. One of my fellow thespies'll see me home."

Voices high with drink, pot, life?

". . . like magic it was . . ."

". . . that second act scene . . ."

". . . the way Jelly shrieked it . . ."

"*I saw Goody* . . ."

". . . appalling . . ."

". . . I mean gutsy . . ."

". . . gutsy . . ."

"Ballsy!"

"... too much, Patrick was just too ..."
"... scotch, scotch rocks ..."
"... bourbon ..."
"... gin ..."
"... Mary Jo ..."
"... Freddy ..."
"... depressing play though, you got to admit ..."
"Hell! Just have that mind-blowin Jelly and, man!"
"... Jack ... hey, Jack, man ..."
The walk to the door was not a short one.

Dream
When you're feeling ...

It was a sparse crowd. No voice in the place rose much above his own, which was so low as to be almost inaudible. "You get 'em early and hold 'em or you don't get 'em," said Jerry Schwartz. Jacob sang one set and left.

It was around three when he got home, having stopped to eat. She wasn't there. Only the sound of silent sleep from the other bedrooms hinted of any life at all in the apartment. He looked in on Billy, who lay imperturbably on his stomach, then he picked up the book nearest his special chair in the living room and—seeing that it contained the teachings of Rabbi Nahman of Bratzlav, the great-grandson of the Baal-Shem Tov—turned in a kind of arch perverseness to the passages on sexual union.

Union represents the state in which breathing is suspended. It is therefore the opposite of the state of longevity, for, as is well known, many people die of this passion. It is also the opposite of wisdom, for many people are driven mad by it. But through the act of union in holiness and purity, life is increased and years are added. Through it "man sees life with his wife" and attains wisdom and elevation of the spirit. Through it . . .

He may have dozed. He didn't think so. Sometimes the profusion of words absorbed at a time when we beg sleep merely passes for it. Whatever, he was startled that it was five o'clock and she still wasn't home. He made himself a cup of instant coffee and laced it generously with brandy, and waited. Billy cried once, in his sleep, around five thirty, but it was quickly gone and unremembered in the stillness. Jelly came in shortly before six.

She was too drunk to speak to; at least to understand. But she made little, if any, noise. If anything, she tiptoed into the bedroom with the kind of exaggerated, whispery silliness that only dreamy drunks can effect. "I saw Goody Jelly with the Devil, Goody Jelly with the Devil, Goody Jelly, Goody Jelly"—over and over in the soft articulateness of unreality.

He managed to get her undressed and to bed. In the darkness (or was light just being born in the morning outside?) she said "Mrs. Jew, Mrs. Jew, Mrs. Rabbi Jew, I told 'em all I was . . . ," and his body was cold even as his imagination burned, and not even her accelerated warmth could induce him to sleep.

Perhaps Sugaree is right, he thought. It *had* been a full moon out tonight. And for them that know its dark side . . .

But then again, as Moses ben Maimon, in the year 1172, said . . .

CHAPTER TWENTY-FIVE

In the morning (it was past noon, actually; Sugaree had already taken Billy to the park), they made love. They didn't so much take each other, respond to each other, as they did incarcerate each other. Their bodies—from short sleep, vengeance, chemistry, love; her painful hangover; his painful thoughts; it didn't matter—were unquenchable. Never had he held an erection so long, never had her juices been so thick and sweet and infinite. They scaled each other, as one scales mountains or canyons, and, crazily challenging each other (even to the point of shouting bets on climax), came together with a kind of prurient grace.

"When Ah's been fucked, Ah's been fucked, and Ah knows Ah's been fucked," she said in a lovely, lonely, deliberately dialectical world away, and he turned on his side in exhausted anguish.

They had little to say to each other in the days and

nights that followed; to do with each other, for that matter. Nights, they performed, rarely even having dinner together, although Sugaree, with a simple but singular artistry, patiently prepared it. Days, she painted, went out; sometimes taking Billy with her, more often leaving him for "play with Day" or the endless island tales of Sugaree. Afternoons, he had taken again to visiting libraries, and more and more frequently the temples and synagogues again, soaking up the healing solitude of sanctuaries as he had the Gulf Coast sun.

There was laughter in the house, of course, but it was usually Billy's.

"They have a most original saying where I am from," Sugaree said to him one day, when they were having a sandwich together for lunch.

"What saying is that?" Jacob asked.

" 'It stink to high heaven,' " she said—airily, knowingly; moving on about her work.

The run of *The Crucible* at Le Petit was extended a week, and they saw each other even less. The play closed on a Saturday night, which called for another cast-and-crew party, this time at the director's apartment on Dauphine, and which he did not attend. She came home, this time both belligerently and aesthetically tight, at dawn.

"Jelly," he said, "we have to right ourselves. I know that sounds old-fash—"

"Screw off."

"For God's sake, Jelly, what are you trying to . . .?"

". . . love you, darlin, I do, I do, why is it all so . . . ?"

"*Goddammit, Jelly, grow up!*"

She simply stared at him with a kind of sad, crooked, drink-thick smile. "There was a time. There was a time, Jack . . ."

A sleepy Billy had opened the door to their bedroom. "Day? What you and Mother . . . ?"

She knelt beside him. "Did it wake you up, Billy Boy? Did your Day's big old voice wake you up? Well, you'll just go right back to sleep, darlin. Right back to gentlin old sleep. And all kinds of good gentlin dreams. And maybe tomorrow, if you're a very good boy, Mother'll tell you all about a beautiful puppy dog she had once, whose name was Isabella of Spain. A long long time ago. You and I are very lucky people, did you know that, Billy Boy? Did you know that? We'll never ever in this world have to worry about Billy Boy's daddy cattin around. You see, in your mother's case, darlin, the other woman is God."

It took every deep breath he could muster to suppress the rage in his chest but Jacob managed, even with a smile, to take the boy in his arms and back to his own room, where he laid him gently back to bed.

"We love you very much, Billy," he said. "Your mother and I. You're our life, son. You're our whole life."

"You're funny," laughed the boy, for no reason except that it was dawn and he was already three-quarters asleep.

When he was again in their room, although his voice was low, Jacob's fury was unmistakable.

"How could you! How in God's name could you! A child, a baby, a . . ."

But she was already face-down on the bed, crying softly but from the deepest recesses of her, and there was nothing for him but to try to comfort her to sleep. Which was a long and exhausting affair, for she wept well into the morning.

It was a Sunday and she left the apartment around noon, several canvases under her arms. He was to meet her at six at Shy's and Andrew P.'s where they were having dinner to celebrate the budding of an actress. She was sullen when she left, quiet and spent, vague about where she would be spending the afternoon, no acknowledgment of the past hours in either her face or her voice. But at Shy's and Andrew P.'s she was electrically alive, garrulously turned on, as indeed was Shy. Their marathon chatter—over Andrew P.'s precious specialty, Chicken and Eggs Sardou, and an "impertinent little wine"—was so obviously induced by something other than natural body chemistry that even Andrew P. said at one point, when he had literally to bull his way in, "While I was slaving over this perfectly gorgeous faggy repast, I have the feeling that *some* people I know were climbing stairways to the stars."

"The stars, the stars, the poor imprisoned stars," laughed Jelly. "Even they've got their *surrus*—is that the word, Jack darlin? Even they've got their fuckin hangups. Whole beautiful infinite solar system and all the kinky cracky earthbound 'stronomers spyin on 'em through their big silly eyeglasses . . ."

And it went on that way.

"A real fun festive evenin," said Shy.

"Just one thing missin," said Jelly. "The Book of Job. My sweet darlin Jacob-Jack, with the blessin in absensha of his salami brother in Dallas and my own dear darlin pork-eatin daddy in Mannerville, will now recite for us the Book of . . ."

Home again, he fumed. "Whatever it is, it's not your grass or pot or whatever you care to call it . . ."

"Careful, darlin. Hard stuff's just sittin there waitin on the stairway to . . ."

"Jelly, we can't go on like this, it's . . ."

"Bein married is crap. Crap! Darlin, let's . . ."

Wearily, unemotionally, he undressed and went to the bathroom to brush his teeth. Within minutes, seconds, she was behind him, naked as he, pressing her fine pubic hair against his buttocks, her arms circling him, finding him, arousing him. They made love, brutally but somehow mechanically, and afterward she said, "Billygoat! Even havin had Billy, my tits are still too small." She wept again.

In desperation, he slept.

CHAPTER TWENTY-SIX

" 'Autumn Leaves,' Jack!"
" 'Blue Room,' Jack!"
" 'Impossible Dream,' Jack!"
" 'Raindrops,' Jack!"
" 'The Lady Is a Tramp,' Jack!"

Mardi Gras, Mardi Gras,
Come on down to Mardi Gras
Grab a gal, grab a guy,
Sing it up, sing it high.
Nothing beams
Like New Orleans
At Mardi Gras.

Mardi Gras . . . Mardi Gras . . .

The Sazerac Room was at capacity; he, however mixed the blessing, at his peak. But his leg ached more than usual, he felt a cold coming on, and had decided to leave early. Lou Rollins, a pianist with the Blue Room orchestra, had agreed to take over.

"One more, Jack!"

"'Strangers in the Night,' Jack!"

"'Raindrops . . .'"

"'Blue Room . . .'"

"'. . . down yonder in . . .'"

He smiled, waved, in his most professional manner, and left. Everywhere, the anticipation of Mardi Gras was in the air again. The hotel lobby, the streets, all were swollen with it. It was still not even midnight. Perhaps he and Jelly could talk, he thought. Sugaree had taken Billy for an overnight visit with a friend in Covington. Perhaps, at last . . .

Strange. He knew, even before he put key to door, that the apartment was swollen with something, too. The dark inside, like carnival itself, was illusory. The muffled laughter from the back bedroom was reality enough.

Perhaps, like childhood, it would recede in his consciousness, dissolving eventually into the thick brown stew of memory. More likely, it was stamped forever in indelible imprint on a brain that would conjure it, day after day, hour upon hour, even to death. Whichever, no sooner had he opened the bedroom door than he closed it, leaving behind it in the dim night light (certain he was seen) the spectacle of Jelly and Shy—straining, unrestrained. Giggling like children with a grand secret.

"Free," she cried out; sang. "Free, fuckin free!"

The words pierced every pore of his body, but because he couldn't see her face, he never saw her tears.

"Free, fuckin free, fuckin free . . ."

Jacob left the apartment without looking back.

They stared curiously, he knew: the tall man with the tears on his face, walking the Quarter streets at such an hour. But it was the time of madness, carnival was only days away, and curiosities at such a time are commonplace.

He had no idea where he was going. Certainly not tonight, much less tomorrow. Or the day after tomorrow. Or the day after that.

Or that.

He simply walked.

After a while, aloud to the night, he said, "You'll be all right, Billy. Even with a bent inheritance, you'll be all right."

Walked.

It was cooler out now, rawer. He had left the apartment without a top coat. He pulled his suit jacket tighter to his neck. Adjusted himself in it. Took a handkerchief from his back pocket and blew his nose. And as he did these things, these simple living physical things; as the Quarter closed in on him like one of Jelly's billygoat freedoms; as from somewhere, from some steamy open doorway, some hundred steamy open doorways, someone, a hundred someones, sang out *Yeh Yeh Yeh, You got to Yeh Yeh Yeh;* as song and place, night and time, met like old but callous friends in his chest; as Jelly herself drifted in and out of his numbed mind like a carnival specter; Jacob found himself recalling—and wryly, even now—an ancient passage from the Talmud, from almost his first boyhood reading of it:

If only they were to forsake me,
and observe my teachings!
WORDS PUT INTO THE MOUTH OF GOD

This book was designed by Irving Perkins,
the type face used is Caledonia
and the books were composed, printed, and bound by
The Book Press, Brattleboro, Vermont.